Fire & Ice:

The Kindred Woods

Book Three

By Erin Forbes

Fire & Ice: The Kindred Woods

Cover Design Copyright © 2018 by Jennifer Zemanek/
Seedlings Design Studio

Map Design Copyright © 2018 by Jennifer Zemanek/
Seedlings Design Studio

First paperback edition 2019

www.fireandicebookseries.com

ISBN-13: 978-0-9997719-4-5 (Hardcover Edition)
ISBN-13: 978-0-9997719-3-8 (Paperback Edition)
ISBN-13: 978-0-9997719-5-2 (E-Book Edition)

For all the wild ones.
You are stronger than you feel,
Braver than you believe,
And wiser than you know.

NORTHERN SEA

N
W   E
S

OUTER ISLES

MACNAS MANOR

THE ACADEMY FOR GIFTED YOUTH

NIGHT OAK FOREST

WILLOWCREST

LENNOX MANOR

The Academy for Gifted Youth

Students

Alice Hanley ~ a lion-hearted girl with
fire in her veins and flames in her heart

Emery Hanley ~ a gentle girl with cerulean eyes and ice in her fingertips

Ariadne Moss ~ her laughter
brings us a gentle breeze

Juniper Stone ~ a wild-haired girl,
whose Gift is as natural as her name

Ronan O'Reilly ~ a freckle-faced
boy with an unbreakable habit of
causing things to levitate

Kade O'Reilly ~ feathered
friend to our heroine

Fionn MacMillan ~ the Lost Dreamer

Violet Holloway ~ a peculiar girl
with lavender hair and eyes that
change color with her emotions

Cleona Lennox ~ a dark-haired girl with a
spiteful personality, better known as Cleo

Grayson Fields ~ a golden-haired
lad with light in his hands

Sage Pine ~ wolf-girl

Hugo Stone ~ the youngest
brother of Juniper Stone

Staff

Zara Hawthorne ~ Headmistress of
the Academy for Gifted Youth

Professor Georgina Iris

Professor Eleanora O'Connor

Sir Theodore Barrington

Ms. Ruby Lane

Ms. Augusta Emerson

Mr. Oliver O' Reilly

Professor Blakely Biddle

The Guardians of Aisling

Killian ~ friend to all freckled creatures

Lachlan ~ the finest archer in Aisling

Niamh ~ the phantom mare; equine
companion of Ronan O'Reilly

Noble Lennox ~ the noble
brother of Cleona Lennox

Emerson ~ an Irish wolfhound
of the most unusual sort

Those who dwell in Aisling...

Willoughby ~ an indecisive old troll who
lives deep within the White Birch Forest

Lydia Ludwig ~ an old woman who lives
on the edge of Willowcrest village

Sir Lennox ~ the wicked father
of the Lennox children

Clara ~ Queen of the Bears

Nicholas Stone ~ the deaf violinist

The Droplet Faeries ~ a species of
tiny faeries who carry water droplets atop their heads and build villages
out of the flowers they tend

The Creatures of the Night Oak Forest ~
invisible to the eye, but not to the mind

Moira & Marina ~ the Siren Sisters

Alexander & Ailsa Hanley ~ the loving
parents of Alice and Emery Hanley

Sir Emerson & Rosemary Holloway ~
the unusual parents of Violet Holloway

Historical Figures of the Realm

Silas Casper ~ founder of the
Academy for Gifted Youth

Wolfgang Gregory ~ responsible for
the curse upon the Night Oak Forest

Orinthia Hanley ~ the late grandmother of the Hanley sisters

Alistair Lennox ~ the late
grandfather of Noble and Cleona

Saoirse MacMillan ~ an innocent girl
lost to the fever; the late sister of Fionn

Kristofer Ó Coileáin ~ a lost love

PROLOGUE

The carriage rattled as we traveled down the forest path, away from the crowded streets of the seaside village. My gaze was settled on the faces of three friends. Our eyes exchanged the expressions of a wordless language, which spoke of the apprehension in our hearts. A pair of strong horses pulled the coach onward, leading us toward an unknown fate.

After the return of the Lost Dreamer, the people of Innis gathered to observe with distinct astonishment. It was quite strange, after all. A teenage boy had replaced the distant memory of a missing child. The news was already beginning to spread across the realm; within a single hour, every person in the surrounding villages had received word of the unusual truth.

The Order of Birch hurried the Four Elementals into a large carriage, which promised to lead us toward the stone walls of Castle Moss. Fionn MacMillan was pushed into the coach that trailed behind us. His family members followed in his footsteps, never daring to let him out of their sight.

At that moment, my heart seemed to burst with a mixture of joy and pity for the MacMillan clan. Fionn's mother was speechless for the entire reunion, as she allowed her fingers to analyze the changes of her son's face. His father reacted with a swell of tears and strong embrace, which promised to protect the lad from further danger. A little girl stood beside her mother, watching this interaction with glazed confusion. Despite their uncanny resemblance, she had never met her famous brother. Even so, she recognized him, for the fair-haired lad once visited her in the land of dreams.

I observed the interaction in silence, allowing emotions to glisten through teardrops. My gown was torn in several places, but the damage did not compare to those scars of the spirit. Images of dark caverns and pale sirens haunted my mind, as though such things were impossible to forget.

Shouts of jubilation flooded the village streets, harmonizing in the form of a single song. While most of the attention was directed toward Fionn, it was no secret that the Four Elementals were responsible for his return. A group of authoritative gazes rested on our shoulders, waiting for a private moment to speak with us. Distinct apprehension pricked at my heart, which warned the guards of my conviction.

As I glanced through the window of the bouncing coach, the villagers watched from the edge of crowded streets. One of my fingers held against the glass, measuring the height of the buildings that continued to shrink as we rushed down the old road. A few friends were left behind in the village, as the Order of Birch didn't have an interest in their connection to the peculiar situation. Killian was forced to board the leading carriage, in company with Professor Hawthorne and the other officials. I was beginning to question the allegiance of each person in life, although the Guardian's loyalty swore to remain steadfast.

The shoreline faded away in the distance, as the carriage passed through the White Birch Forest. A haze of emerald leaves and gnarled trees painted across the glass. The horses trotted over the light that pierced through the canopy of trees.

In time, the carriage rounded the turn beside the walls of Castle Moss. The stone fortress was surrounded by prim hedges and flowering trees. The road was deserted, as if the Gifted people had been ordered to keep their distance. A single knight stood in front of the unbreakable doors, waiting, waiting for us to arrive. A silver sword was slung into the scabbard on his waist. His right hand clenched around the handle, ready for a chance to prove his worth.

As the carriage slowed down, each of the passengers glanced through the window. Ariadne rolled her eyes, as though she didn't understand the need for such theatrics. My twin sister, Emery, allowed her fingertips to frost with the unease of her expression. Juniper Stone did not reveal the emotions in her heart; rather, she watched with careful attention to the details of her surroundings.

The door swung open as a pair of armored knights appeared beside the coach. The headmistress held the handle, accompanied by the familiar faces of Lachlan and Killian. She offered patience and trust. As we stepped out of the carriage, the knights turned to stand on both sides. We walked toward the entrance of the ancient castle, which governed the entire realm.

My gown had dried with the warmth of the fire in my veins. My sister was soaked in the water of the Northern Sea, her blonde hair slicked back from her pale face. A touch of pink spread across her cheeks, vanishing at the tip of her nose. As the castle doors opened wide, she stared forward with flickering eyes.

A marble floor spread out before us, leading to a stairwell in the middle of the entrance hall. A pair of single doors were built into the walls on both sides. The stones were decorated with tapestries that depicted elements of Gifted folklore. A banner of the realm was displayed above the window at the crown of the staircase.

We strode through the narrow halls, which seemed to continue for an eternity. Each footstep penetrated through the deafening silence, daring to wake an invisible beast from hibernation. Not a single person walked through the abandoned corridors.

The headmistress came to a halt beside a red doorway, which shimmered with a fresh coat of paint. She placed her fingers on the golden handle, gesturing for us to follow her inside. The room contained a large study, although not a single book rested on the shelves that lined the walls. Bottles of unrecognizable substances were displayed in place of novels and field guides. An occasional scroll or piece of parchment was placed beside the objects. A large desk stood on the other side of the room, accompanied by five chairs for the interrogation.

That was the reason we were here, after all.

The Order of Birch waited to dissect each thought that flowed through our individual minds. In the opinion of the officials, we were nothing more than a group of rebellious teenagers with dangerous powers. Even so, we had managed to accomplish a great deal in the past year.

A tall man walked into the room. Despite the circumstances, his expression was grim. Although we had never met before, his identity was not difficult to guess. My thoughts flashed back to the letter received from Castle Moss. The man was known as Bastian Amulet—President of the Order of Birch.

As I settled into a chair, each of the others imitated me. Saltwater and sand formed puddles around their toes. The Lost Dreamer claimed his seat in the middle of the group, before his parents were swiftly escorted away from the room.

"Good afternoon," said Bastian. "I expect you must be wondering the reason we called all of you here."

The man's skin resembled a wrinkled prune, dark and withered from lack of care. His hair was touched by the silver mark of age, although his eyes gleamed with an unusually bright expression. His gaze seemed to linger on the worrisome countenance of Fionn MacMillan. Despite his authoritative position, the unfortunate chains of mistrust were bound to the man's character.

"We are less suspicious than you might expect," I responded. "Perhaps you would care to explain."

My gaze drifted toward Professor Hawthorne, who stood beside the desk with Killian. She had not spoken a word since our return to the village, and such a distant attitude was uncharacteristic. The blurred lines of division were beginning to emerge, and trust was not granted with ease.

"Well," replied Bastian, "as I'm sure you can imagine, the discovery of the Lost Dreamer was quite unexpected."

"Really?" Ariadne inquired, allowing her voice to reveal a hint of sarcasm. "That explains the Guardians who greeted us in the town square, prepared to carry us off to Castle Moss."

"Please, girls," Zara spoke at last. "Be civil."

"You're *not* my mother," Ariadne retorted.

"That's true, but you must learn to take orders from the headmistress of the Academy for Gifted Youth," stated Bastian. "Before the information was shared with us, we did not know about your quest to find Fionn MacMillan."

"You speak as if he isn't here," said Juniper, gesturing to the silent dreamer.

My gaze rested on Bastian's unsettled character. The corners of his bearded mouth twitched with discomfort, as if his expression struggled to remain neutral. He was scared. As my eyes followed the man's hesitant glances, a peculiar realization dawned upon me. The most powerful man in the entire realm of Aisling had developed an unexplainable fear of the Gifted children seated before him.

"The Academy for Gifted Youth will be open for education in less than a month," said Bastian. "Although classmates will be aware of the lad's return, I must forbid the discussion of further information. This is a matter of significance to the Order of Birch, and it shall not be shared with the general population. A single rumor can spread like wildfire in these parts of the realm."

"Oh, trust me," I murmured. "Nothing spreads like a wildfire."

A deafening silence settled across the room, crawling over the smooth surface of the desk. It nestled into empty bookshelves, between the old scrolls and glass vials. Although my words spoke only the truth, such a statement was bound to be considered a threat.

My eyes flashed toward Killian. The little red fox watched me with careful attention. He was settled at the foot of the headmistress. In another form, the Guardian would have towered several inches above the regal woman. Something hid behind the twitch of his ears and the anxious flick of his russet tail.

The silence shattered with the words of the headmistress, as she turned to question her students about the heroic quest. We spoke about the visions and nightmares that connected my sister to the sorrows and troubles of the Lost Dreamer. The words escaped with careful hesitation, as no one dared to share the details.

Eyes of suspicion burned through the countenance of every child in the room. A few were wise enough to meet the gaze with courage, while others stared at the lacing of their boots.

There was a strange feeling in my core, which seemed to warn of an unknown threat. A flicker of golden sparks danced across my fingertips. Perhaps it was the voice of my flames, attempting to guard a piece of fate.

In my imagination, the Order of Birch was a fellowship of wise elders, working together for the protection of the realm. But the truth dared to emerge from the fog of childhood. The bookshelves of this study were created to hold works of brilliance. My grandmother, Orinthia, once stood behind the desk. She sought to govern the Gifted people with justice and compassion. The Order of Birch had changed in a matter of years. A strange darkness nestled in its core, infecting each member with lack of conscience.

As questions trailed off into silence, the headmistress met my gaze. A thin veil covered her intentions, and all traces of emotion were stripped from her smile. I searched for a message in her sapphire eyes, hoping to reassure the shaken image of her character. Zara Hawthorne had earned so much of my trust, and it wasn't difficult to believe she deserved it. But there she was, standing beside a man of opposite worth and character.

"What do you want from us?" I demanded.

"Nothing," said Bastian. "We seek to understand the situation. After all, it's rather curious. I can only wonder how the answers slipped through my mind."

The man lied. I could see it in his eyes, the way his gaze wandered from left to right. Something told me that he knew all about the mysterious disappearance of the Lost Dreamer. It would be foolish to place my trust in his hands, and I was not a foolish girl.

"There is only one way to escape this matter," said Bastian. "We must move forward."

I remained silent, glancing toward my sister. The fair-haired girl stared at the man, analyzing the details of his peculiar face. Her focus dared to shatter every piece of glass in the castle. After a long moment, she narrowed her eyes and turned to look at me. Emery was unable to read his intentions, although she did not seem surprised. She blinked away the trace of suspicion in her cerulean gaze.

The Order of Birch wanted to erase the mysteries of the past, the secrets that washed in with the tide. A hidden truth lingered between each member of their society. Amulet looked down upon the children in front of him, as though youth were an irrefutable sign of folly. Unlike the headmistress, he was cold and distant. The man did not sympathize with Fionn's tale, as he was more concerned about keeping his return discreet.

My train of thought was interrupted by a sudden knock on the door. Killian pricked his ears forward, listening to the footsteps that paced outside the chamber.

"Well then." Bastian sighed, waving his hand in a circular motion. "You are dismissed. The knights will lead you out to the carriage, which will return to Macnas Manor."

I did not speak a word before standing up and walking toward the door. The red fox trotted close to my heels,

9

matched by the strides of our Gifted companions. The once intriguing castle was beginning to feel more like a prison. Beautiful tapestries and innocent hearts were pointless in such a place. My skin longed to be reunited with the warm summer breeze. As a pair of knights held the door open, golden sparks leaped from my fingertips.

A familiar, dark-haired man paced between the corridors. His eyebrows furrowed in a thoughtful expression. His regal attire was comparable to that of a foreign king. As I swept across the floor, his shadowed gaze burned into me.

Emery grabbed my hand as the man marched into the room. "Sir Lennox," she whispered. "What is he doing here?"

The armored knights slammed the door behind them. I flinched at the sudden sound, which echoed down the halls. The reverberations seemed to swallow the place all at once. My gaze settled on the large frame that hung over the doorway, depicting the aged portrait of Professor Silas Casper. The Academy founder rattled against the walls, which promised to keep the secrets spoken on the other side.

CHAPTER ONE

Blue waves crashed against the shore, sprinkling water droplets across my toes. The laughter of Gifted people filled my ears, daring to burst through tangled thoughts. My bare feet were planted firmly in the white sand, as if the wind dared to carry me away. The beach was scattered with parents and students of all ages. Their soft voices traveled across the breeze, which carried the joyful songs of the Late Summer Festival.

A week had passed since the return of Fionn MacMillan; however, so much had changed. The stares of classmates and professors followed me with the persistence of shadows. It was impossible to avoid the whispers that settled in my wake. The curiosity of the villagers was evident, even while few dared to voice their inquiries. As time passed, the trail of murmurs blended with the melody of nature. My head no longer turned to identify the speakers.

Flowering dreams replaced the nightmares that faded away from hours of sleep. A subconscious comfort returned to my nonsensical imagination, which provided a sanctuary for restless thoughts. The visions carried me to a land of boundless nature and vivid color, covering my mind in a blanket of silk.

I watched as a silver dragonfly soared over the rippling tide. Its crystal wings fluttered faster than the speed of light, although each motion was made with care and precision. Glittering eyes protruded from the face of the flying insect, which observed the realm from an unknown perspective. The creature did not recognize my freckled face and flaming hands; it did not even care to regard my presence. I found reassurance in the ethereal silence.

"Alice?" a voice spoke from behind me.

After a moment of hesitation, I turned toward a familiar face. *Ronan O'Reilly.* The shine of his smile was masked by the crease between his dark brows. A spark of happiness contrasted the worried look in his gaze.

"Hello, Ronan," I responded, before turning back toward the raging sea.

"Are you well?" the lad inquired.

"Oh, yes!" I sighed. "I'm fine."

"Have you decided to abandon the festivities of the gathering?" my friend persisted. "I don't blame you—the crowd can be quite overbearing."

"You speak the truth," I replied, attempting to hide my amusement. "Even so, the other students have not cared enough to interrupt my precious solitude."

A grin spread across Ronan's freckled cheeks, curving around that single dimple on the right side of his face. The boy never failed to lift my spirit. Although I did not know it at the time, my dear friend was falling from a terrible height.

"Do not linger on the shores of the past, Alice," Ronan said, stepping into the forest of my mind. "You deserve to move forward with courage and strength."

Everyone begged me to move forward, but the past called for my attention. It carried the hope of the future.

I felt a tug on the sleeve of my gown. The fabric lifted around my wrists and pulled toward the lad. As I refused to regard his childish request, Ronan strode across the sand. His smile did not fade with the roll of my eyes.

"Follow me," he insisted. "Your friends have been looking for you, and they are going to wonder where you've been. The celebration lacks a certain essence without you."

"You're such a child." I laughed, allowing him to lead me away from the water.

The conversation of our classmates seemed to blossom as we neared the giant marquee tent. An old fiddle provided our spirits with a joyful tune, and people of all ages twirled across the floor. I caught sight of a familiar smile in the midst of the crowd.

My sister's dress flowed in a circle around her waist, like a fresh morning glory against a wall of vines. Laughter and incandescence beamed from her face, which directed my attention to her partner. Despite his many years spent away from society, Fionn had developed into a proper gentleman. He was a loyal friend to each of the Four Elementals.

"It seems like your sister has found a steadfast companion," said Ronan, noticing the center of my focus. "Fionn is quite the remarkable dancer."

"Perhaps," I responded, addressing his first statement. "But they are nothing more than friends."

"Of course," said Ronan. "Just like us."

"Yes," I responded, tripping over the simple word. Despite the overwhelming urge to meet his blue eyes, my gaze lingered on the sand that covered our bare feet. Amidst the swirling haze of colors, a collection of crystal clear emotions dared to break free.

As we walked through the scattered groups of people, glowing embers danced between my strands of hair. A few people turned to stare, although each gaze held the comfort of admiration. My skin did not crawl with the sensation of being watched like a curious beast in a circus. My thoughts drifted back to memories of my first presentation in front of the Academy for Gifted Youth. One year ago, my life changed, and the reality of such magic was inconceivable. The transformation dared to continue for an eternity; however, I was learning to find solace in the peculiarities of my soul.

"Alice!" a light voice called. "We have been searching for you."

I lifted my head to greet the smiling faces of Juniper Stone and Ariadne Moss. The two girls sat beside one of the white tea tables. Countless seashells were spread out across the surface, shimmering in the light of the golden afternoon. A familiar child lingered nearby, begging to braid through the tangles of Juniper's mane.

"Don't touch it," Ariadne warned. "If you add a single trace of color, she will never forgive you. Trust me, Holland. You don't want to experience such a wrath."

As the young girl laughed, her identity flooded back to mind. Holland Shepherd possessed the talent of giving color to the dullest of flowers. She provided much entertainment in my first year at the Academy for Gifted Youth. When the student was not giggling with her friends, she extracted the garish dye from the gowns in Ruby Lane's wardrobe. Her mischievousness was an innocent light behind the rising shadows of the realm.

A group of children hurried across the dance floor, running between couples and knocking into professors. Melodies of laughter followed in their wake, accompanied by a wispy trail of fabric. One of the little girls tagged Holland on the shoulder, prompting her to abandon the elder students. As she followed in the footsteps of her friends, flurries of brilliant color exploded into the air.

Juniper waved her hand toward the empty chair, gesturing for me to take a seat. I followed her command in silence, focusing on the seashells scattered over the tea table.

My thoughts returned to the Lost Dreamer; after all, so much of his childhood was wasted in the cavern under the sea. The fair-haired boy was unable to hide the scars that accompanied his past. He deserved to stand on the shore with peace in his heart. Despite the radiance of his smile, it was clear that he struggled to adjust. His portrait was plastered on the walls of every shop in the village, and his name was present in each statement of local gossip. Every person in the realm of Aisling was familiar with his tale.

The Gifted students were scheduled to move back to the Academy in less than a week. Although the thought delighted my spirit, it never failed to remind me of the change that would be present. Stone castles and flowering courtyards remained the same, but a distinct difference was destined to be discovered in the eyes of close companions.

Ariadne stifled a burst of laughter as she stared across the crowd, toward the center of the celebration. I followed her gaze, eventually settling on the figure that approached. Emery glided toward us, unaware of the sheet of ice that she left behind. As the next quadrille began, unfortunate couples slipped across the floor. Despite shouts of annoyance, the girl remained oblivious. For once in her lifetime, Emery's pale cheeks were tinted the color of fresh roses. A delicate smile settled across her lips.

"Emery," said Juniper. "You're blushing."

"On the contrary," replied Emery, lifting the fabric around her ankles. "I'm merely flushed. Fionn is an enthusiastic dancer, and this gown is much too heavy for the summer months."

Ariadne and Juniper exchanged a glance before returning their attention to the collection on the table. The former dunked each of the seashells into a small bowl of water, attempting to cleanse away the sand. The latter placed the sparkling curios into a large basket. Vines twisted around the handle, as though the wood had been plucked from the depths of the forest.

"What are you doing?" I inquired.

"We are preparing the basket for the ceremony of hopes and sorrows," Juniper replied. "It is an annual tradition of the Late Summer Festival."

"The seashells are passed around the gathering, until each person has one to represent the greatest sorrows and fears in their heart," Ariadne explained. "As the shells are tossed into the ocean, the people seek to find solace."

After a few moments, the final shell was placed into the basket. Juniper stood up and dusted her gown before gesturing for us to take our pick from the collection. The conversation of the festival fell into silence, as the Gifted people drifted away from the marquee. A large gathering formed near the edge of the water, where students and professors stood barefoot in the sand.

"Well," said Ariadne. "We must follow them."

The petite girl skipped away from the tea table, before twirling across the empty dancefloor. Her short hair tossed around her cheeks, as the late summer wind rushed through the air. A sharp and impatient attitude was abandoned in the laughter that trailed behind her.

Emery glanced at me with wide eyes before Juniper grabbed our hands and followed after the crowd. A crown of wildflowers began to bloom around her forehead. Although I was unable to find the source of the blossoms, it was not difficult to imagine the stems grew out of her mind.

17

I turned the seashell in my hand, imagining the strong waves that had formed its shape.

"My mother once told me," Juniper said, "if the seashell skips across the water, a great wish will come true."

After a moment, the wild-haired girl kissed the shining object in her hand. She opened her eyes against a bright smile, which reflected the unfathomable dreams in her heart. As a gentle wave crashed upon the shore, Juniper tossed her shell into the Northern Sea. It skipped across the water before falling under the foaming waves.

Ariadne did not take a second glance before throwing her token into the sea. While it did not skip across the reflective tide, the ocean swallowed it with a promise. Thousands of unknown hopes and sorrows fell under the surface.

I rotated the silver shell in my hand, pondering the dreams that I wished to place with it. Recent worries had been exchanged with unexplainable suspicion, which was to be addressed at another time and place. The history of Aisling developed an important position in the back of my mind, and the topic never failed to enter my train of thought.

In this truth, my wish was discovered. Finding the courage to set it free, I watched it skip across the tide.

CHAPTER TWO

The next few days swept away with the summer tide. Despite many efforts to focus on different matters, my mind was settled on the mysteries of the past. So many questions remained unanswered.

As I wandered through the corridors of Macnas Manor, the dawn light drifted through the windows. Morning fog settled over the meadows, which stretched far beyond my little corner of the realm. A nightgown swayed above my bare feet, imitating the dance of the woodland faeries. Not a single voice was heard in the empty halls, as the hour was too early for a proper night of rest. I did not care enough to sleep. Daylight hours promised a wealth of interaction, but solitude never failed to provide a renewed sense of peace.

Loneliness is a very strange thing. In the perfect setting, it can bring a soft comfort to the human spirit, yet it also has the power to pull one to the ground. For the moment, I was satisfied with the former, and such freedom ignited sparks in my tangled hair.

The old manor felt a bit more like the farmhouse I had left behind in New England. Of course, the stone walls and hidden passageways proved regal, but it was difficult to compete with the house of childhood. In many ways, my family had carried the meaning of home to Aisling. It was found in the radiance of my mother's smile and the blue eyes of my father. Memories of my grandmother lingered in every corner of the manor, as though her words were unable to part from this realm.

Silent footsteps carried me aimlessly down the hall. My lips smacked together every few moments, as I recited the lines of a favored sonnet. The words clung to the edge of my teeth, whispering in the rhythm of poetry. My ancestors watched behind the faded portraits that lined the walls. A few of those individuals had developed a passion for literature, although my grandmother was the only one to pursue it.

When the final stanza was spoken, I entered the spare room at the end of the hall. Golden sunlight streamed through the windows, illuminating the dust that blanketed the floor. Not a single piece of furniture adorned the empty chamber.

As I stepped across the creaking wood, my gaze settled on the little book in the center of the room. The old volume had not been touched since my previous visit, yet it seemed to capture the entire essence of the house. I fell to my knees on the powdered floor. Ginger curls tumbled over my shoulders, dusting the surface of the scarlet binding. I lifted the cover of the old novel and rediscovered the iron key between those hollowed pages.

I glanced over my shoulder for a moment before grabbing the object and closing the book. It was not much of a secret, but I did not care to be followed. The forgotten library called for attention, and I was not afraid to walk alone. An old lantern perched on the windowsill, guarding the keyhole to a secret passage. A single ember escaped my grasp before igniting the kerosene.

It was not long before I dropped into the darkness between the floorboards. Luckily, it was expected this time, but that mere fact did not prevent a terrible scream. I landed beside an intricate display of cobwebs, which burned in the foreign light of my flames.

Dusting off my nightgown, I wandered down the tenebrous path. My light footsteps were the only traces of sound, as my father's snores faded into the distance. Shadows dared to consume the entire realm. My gaze trailed across the arches that maintained the structure of the forgotten tunnel. I noticed the white frost that covered the wood in a swirling pattern. My fair-haired sister was sure to be sleeping in the chamber above my head.

When I reached the entrance to my grandmother's library, the faint scent of lavender lingered in the air. Contentment washed over my senses, while distinct childhood memories returned to mind. I stepped through the open doorway with hesitation, taking in the sight of the familiar writing desk. Papers scattered across the floor. A tweed jacket collected dust over the back of the chair. Tears welled up in my eyes, but I refused to release the flood of emotions.

Not long before my seventh birthday, that woman had traveled to our former home in New England. She arrived late in the afternoon, when the sun set over the emerald fields. Songbirds hushed as she strode down the road. Although I did not know it at the time, she had traveled through the same portal that brought me to the Gifted realm.

Orinthia greeted my father with dramatic delight, for she always regarded him with the affection due to a small child. The tall man never seemed to mind. I stood on the porch with my twin sister, listening to the sound of the woman's rapt voice. When she parted from the warm embrace, she turned her attention to the feminine figure that loomed behind me. Orinthia dropped her luggage in the grass and reached for the hands of my gentle mother. A burst of laughter shattered the silence. Her eyes sparkled with happiness as she gathered her granddaughters into her arms. As I swung around her shoulders, that floral perfume filled my senses.

Pulling my focus back to the present moment, I wandered over to the bookshelves that lined the walls of the hidden chamber. My fingers ran over the leather binding of the novels. One of the volumes was adorned with a golden cover, which shimmered in the light of my flames. As I pulled it away from the collection, a groan sounded from behind the walls. A sharp breath escaped my lungs, settling on the conclusion that all proper libraries include a trace of everlasting magic.

I stopped in my tracks, noticing the second floor that towered overhead. There was no visible access from the main floor of the study. A faint light gleamed between a crack in the corner of the bookshelves. As I peeked through the fracture in the polished wood, the sunrise drifted through a window on the other side. A spiraling staircase stood beside the lunette, reaching toward the second floor of the library.

Precious stories dwelled in the restricted space. I was determined to discover a path of entrance. Before glancing back at the golden book, a sudden realization dawned upon me.

"Of course!" I exclaimed.

That old volume was the key to the concealed stairwell. As I pulled the binding out of line, the hardwood floor began to tremble. Bookshelves shifted to reveal the hidden room.

Illustrated fairytales and folklore filled the space between each of the bookshelves on the second floor. A familiar line of handwriting was scrawled across the front page of the novella in my hands. I traced the lines with my fingers, hoping to gain an impression from the ink.

"Alice," a rough voice spoke from behind me.

I jumped with surprise, turning to meet the eyes of my father. His expression was kind and almost delighted, but I was unable to slow my racing heartbeat.

"I'm not surprised to find you here," the man spoke, allowing a trickle of laughter to fall between his lips. "Your curiosity lacks borders."

"I'm sorry," I responded with a careful smile.

"No need to apologize, my dear girl," he replied before taking the book from my hands. His blue gaze faltered at the sight of the calligraphy. After a long moment, he closed the cover and stared at the title. "This was one of my favorite childhood storybooks... *The Tale of Forgotten Mermaids*."

My thoughts turned their attention to the sight of the author's name. "O.A. Hanley," I murmured.

"Yes," said Father. "Orinthia Ariella Hanley... your grandmother was the famous authoress."

He stared at me with humble amusement. "You are welcome to read all of the books in this collection. I believe they have been untouched for far too long," he spoke, returning the publication to my hands. "Each story was created to be shared with the world, and I know your grandmother wanted to share each word with you."

"Thank you," I responded, "so very much."

"The pen provides a pathway for the musings of the heart," he replied with a smile.

My father descended the stairwell, leaving me in the comfort of the boundless library. I followed soon after, before glancing through the large window at the end of the spiraling steps. A jar of daylight poured like fresh honey over the land. The forest illuminated in a golden glow, which roused the woodland creatures from a deep slumber.

A lone fox waited on the edge of the tree line, watching the manor with a thoughtful expression. His russet tail flicked across the emerald grass. There was no doubt it was Killian, my fierce and loyal guardian. He was often spotted near the edge of Macnas Manor, watching over the Hanley residence. I didn't always see him, but I knew he was always there.

CHAPTER THREE

September arrived with a burst of fresh flowers and rain showers. I found myself seated in a little white house, which nestled on the edge of the village of Willowcrest. A familiar typewriter was settled in the corner of the drawing room. The ink-covered papers were arranged in a neat pile on the desk, where poetry and prose contrasted notes of influence. A pair of birds chirped in a silver cage beside the open window.

A gathering of ladies surrounded the curly-haired woman in the center of the room. She was dressed in an ivory gown and a crown of peonies. Her gap-toothed smile seemed to shine with an irreplaceable brilliance.

"Oh, Augusta," said Emery. "You are positively radiant!"

"Thank you, lovely," Augusta replied, tucking a strand of hair behind her elvish ears. "I really must thank all of you for being here. I would not have been able to settle for any other group of bridesmaids."

"Well," I responded, "you deserve the best, and I'm not sure my affections would endure the heartbreak of another option."

A burst of laughter spread across the room. It lifted the corners of our lips, forming crinkles at the edges of our eyes. A haze of lilac ribbons and braids rippled through the room as Juniper Stone and Violet Holloway danced across the floor. In the harmony of merriment, the purity of friendship and sisterhood was found. When a light knock sounded at the doorway, the voices fell into a curious silence.

"Yes?" Augusta called.

"The guests are arriving," a familiar voice spoke as the door opened in a creak of hesitation.

As Juniper pinned an abundance of flowers between my tangled curls, a childish smile spread across her cheeks. My eyebrows furrowed in confusion as she dropped the lily in her left hand. She flashed an emerald wink over my head.

Ronan stood in the entrance, staring across the room with a far-off expression. He swayed in his boots for a moment before adjusting his collar. Deep oceans and cloudless skies imitated the color of his eyes.

"Well then." Augusta sighed. "My lovely ladies are dismissed."

The Gifted women rushed through the open doors, keen to soak in the festivities of the wedding. A trail of pastel fabric and lace flowed behind them. When the corridor cleared, the lad had vanished.

Juniper retrieved the fallen flower and pinned it behind her ear. As the sound of footsteps faded into the distance, she hummed a light-hearted tune. She finished her work with the enthusiasm of an artist. Each strand of hair was tucked back in an intricate style. After swiping a hint of blush on my cheeks, the wild-haired girl held a mirror to my face.

I stared at my reflection for a long moment. The crown of nature had transformed me into an unknown queen. Even so, it was not difficult to recognize the features of my freckled countenance. Under all of the flourishes and frills, a teenage girl waited for the future.

Perhaps I'd stand in this position in the future, with a white gown and veil to cover those curls of mine.

As I stood up from the vanity chair, my balance teetered on towering heels. Juniper watched for a moment before removing the uncomfortable footwear. "There you are, Alice." She laughed, tossing the heels across the room. "In my opinion, shoes are entirely unnecessary."

"You are a very curious girl," I replied after noticing bare feet under the hem of her gown. My words spoke only the truth, and she did not seem to mind. Unlike so many, the girl never lost her childish freedom and imagination.

"All people are curious," said Juniper, "but most are quite skilled at hiding it."

"There is value in such a trait," I remarked. "A courageous spirit is needed to tend the mind with care."

Before we turned to walk out the door, the girl dared to glance into my soul. She seemed to notice the faint scars, which continued to heal over untended wounds. A glimmering light shone from the little fractures, revealing the hope that guarded me.

"You are a courageous girl," Juniper said. "Never forget the beauty of your power. When life seems comparable to a broken tea cup, one must realize there is nothing more than a single chip in the porcelain."

"Juniper," said Ariadne, peeking around the corner at the end of the hall. "You speak words of nonsense."

"I have learned from the language of flowers," she replied.

After a bit of laughter, we followed after the others. The sharp tune of a fiddle drifted through the air, while delicate shadows danced across the walls. Gifted children and adults wandered through the narrow corridors. Although the little home was old-fashioned, a trace of magic remained in each corner.

A large gathering mingled in the main room of the house. It poured through the open doors. As I stood before the crowd, familiar faces turned to glance at me.

"Alice Hanley!"

A few shouts of surprise sounded as the crowd parted to reveal a winged girl. With a careless smile, she dashed between her fellow students. Strong wings dared to lift her off the ground before she crashed into me with the embrace of true friendship.

"Kade!" A burst of laughter escaped me. "I was looking for you this morning. Where have you been? I caught a glimpse of your brother, but he did not remain long enough to speak with me."

"I was helping my mother with the decorations," the girl replied. "That woman has been so anxious about my uncle's wedding, and the couple assigned her with several tasks. Oliver and Augusta have no interest in the details."

"Your uncle is fortunate to have such a careful sister," I responded, watching the brown-haired woman from the other side of the room. Mrs. O'Reilly was wrapped in a cheerful conversation with my mother. As the ladies exchanged glances of amusement, words of unknown significance glided between them.

"Sometimes," Kade whispered, "I wonder about the words spoken between our mothers."

"Perhaps you should inquire," a sonorous voice spoke from behind me.

I turned to greet Ronan's dimpled smile. The lad was dressed in formal attire and shining leather boots. He stepped closer as the conversation shifted, and breath caught in my chest.

"Hello, Alice," he said, regarding my presence with a respectful nod.

"Where have you been wandering?" I inquired.

"Around," Ronan responded, plucking a few stray feathers from the wings of his twin sister. Kade swiftly countered this action with a gentle punch in her brother's side.

After a while, the bustle of conversation settled down, and the celebration trickled into the outdoors. The fresh scent of flowers swept across the late summer breeze, revealing the earliest traces of autumn. A light path directed our footsteps toward the woodland, where a stream gurgled through the tree roots.

Juniper ran her fingers along the trunks of passing sycamores. The branches seemed to reach out for her attention, while buds opened in her wake.

❧❧❧

When the ceremony ended, the gathering melted away from the hollow between the trees. Long vines dangled from the branches overhead, and enchanted lanterns illuminated the shadows of the woodland path. Dashing between the scattered flower petals, the married couple rushed down the aisle. A stableman stood at the end of the white carpet, holding the reins of a noble steed. Oliver leaped on the back of the horse before sweeping his bride into the saddle with him.

Laughter and applause echoed through the forest grove, while the couple cantered into the distance. Augusta's veil waved in the breeze, guiding the celebration to the tent of the reception.

"She must have the blood of faeries in her veins," Kade murmured. "I've never seen such happiness in her eyes."

"Augusta has found her match." I smiled. "She deserves such a gentleman."

"Your uncle's childish delight has spread to the soul of a dear friend," Juniper said. "It provides a gentle reminder that imagination must not be abandoned."

As I wandered away from the rows of chairs, the remainder of the guests followed hoof prints into the distance. Their faint melodies and shouts of banter traveled over the breeze. Glowing lanterns accompanied the Gifted people, urging me to follow the trail of flames.

Juniper and Ariadne sauntered over the moss-covered earth, before stepping into the carriage that waited on the path. As my bare feet carried me down the aisle, a bloom of tulle fabric swayed around my toes. A moment passed before I noticed the details of my surroundings. Countless petals were beginning to rise above the ground, forming the figures of curious creatures. Floral dragons swept through the air, each one breathing out a burst of fallen petals. A phoenix formed from these imitations of fire, before soaring over my head.

"Such a love is worthy of admiration," Ronan commented. His words spoke nothing more than the simple truth, as pure intentions lingered in the hearts of the couple.

A group of droplet faeries marveled at the petals that floated above their heads. A young female stood with her basket in hand, watching the forage escape her grasp. Even so, she did not seem vexed, for she turned to watch me with a smile.

CHAPTER FOUR

The next day arrived with ease, as I blinked against the light of dawn. Droplets of rain were scattered across the window, reminding me of the night before. A terrible storm disturbed those hours of sleep. Flashes of lightning triggered memories of a dark-haired girl with a sharp temper. There was power behind her black eyes, which dared to strike the Gifted people.

I glanced toward the nightstand, pushing the strange vision into the back of my mind. A steaming cup of tea waited for my attention. I slipped out of bed and picked up the delicate piece of porcelain. A spoon balanced on the edge, dripping with honey. A warm smile spread across my lips, before taking a sip of the tea.

My mother was already out in the garden. She admired the unusual flowers that twirled around the gate. A small bucket hung from her right arm, which carried recycled seeds from her favorite blossoms. Her strawberry-blonde hair contrasted the green plants and pale flowers that remained.

I glanced in the mirror. A mess of curls flowed over my shoulders, begging to be cleansed in fresh water. It was difficult to ignore my insecurities in such a state; however, those thoughts were distracted by matters of more importance. As I pushed open the window panes, a whisper of autumn swept over the land. It rattled the branches of a distant birch forest, where sunlight painted the leaves in gold.

"Good morning, Alice."

I turned to see a pair of blue eyes peeking through a crack in the doorway. The wood groaned as it opened to reveal my twin sister.

"I'm surprised to see you awake," Emery remarked.

"I did not sleep long," I responded. "The storm was loud and frightful. Oh, I sound like a child!"

"Well, you are," said Emery, "both a young woman and child… and there is wonder in such a truth."

I stared at my sister for a moment, noticing the changed details of her face. The angle of her chin was smooth and thin, and her eyes were rounder than before. She was no longer a little girl, but the spirit of youth remained. Perhaps she noticed the same transformation in me.

"There is much to do," said Emery. "As you know, we leave tomorrow."

A smile spread across my lips with the mere thought of returning to the Academy for Gifted Youth. The scent of old books and enchanted classrooms filled my heart with delight. Even so, time brought many changes, and things were different than before.

"Are you looking forward to it?" I inquired.

"Of course," Emery replied. "Aren't you?"

"Yes," I murmured. "I'm longing to step foot in the castle, but I have been troubled since our meeting with the Order of Birch. My regard for Professor Hawthorne has swayed a bit."

"Your trust is an honor," said Emery. "Sometimes, it can be difficult to know who is worthy… but you can place your secrets on my shoulders. And I know you can find the same assurance in Killian, Juniper, and Ariadne."

"Loyal friendships are irreplaceable," I murmured, before meeting her eyes with a faint smile.

My attention turned to the empty trunk beside the bedroom door. A few textbooks were tossed against the wood, collecting dust between dog-eared pages. The rest of my belongings waited to be packed away, as the time of departure approached.

"Tomorrow," I whispered, allowing the word to slip away from me.

It was quite strange to think about the past, which was soon to be replaced by the hopeful future. As I walked across the floor, the creaking wood transformed into polished marble. Memories of bright lanterns and conversations lingered. My heart ached for the solace found behind castle walls.

The rest of the morning was spent between the doors of my wardrobe. Countless gowns and riding breeches were placed between piles of books.

"Where did you find this?" Emery inquired, picking up the old storybook that our father had given me.

"Oh, isn't it marvelous?" I replied. "It was nestled on a hidden floor of the library, which I accessed through a passage between one of the shelves."

Emery examined the book for a few minutes, allowing her fingers to trail across the name of the author. She smiled with recognition. "I should have known it was her work," she whispered.

Overcome with curiosity, my attention drifted away from the mess of clothing. As my sister flipped through the illustrated pages, she hummed an unknown tune. Fair mermaids with sapphire scales surrounded the lines of ink. Each word spoke of sisterhood, sorrow, and betrayal.

I caught sight of the strange splotches that stained the corner of a single page. Emery did not seem to notice, as she continued to move the papers.

"Wait." I slammed my hand down on the book.

Emery was startled, but the expression soon faded as her gaze settled on the spots. It was a rare shade of beryl ink, which could only be traced back to the writing desk in our grandmother's chamber. Such a mishap was not characteristic of the authoress—her careful nature dwelled in every trace of her actions.

My sister placed her finger on the paper. A single word and pair of identical letters was encircled by the same ink that stained the corner of the page. Morning light poured through the open window, which illuminated the shadowed corner of the room.

"Tell..." Emery said, allowing her voice to shatter the silence. "L.L."

The fair-haired girl turned to look at me. Her cerulean eyes searched for a hint of understanding. Stillness settled back into the manor. The only sound was the soft laughter of sparrows. It was a message, the strange secret that hid behind letters.

I placed a marker between the pages, releasing a sigh of frustration. Our grandmother had a knack for leaving questions in her wake, and the Elementals were destined to find the answers. The Gifted society was wrapped in a blanket of secrets, which dared to suffocate the treasures of individualism. My intuition whispered against the hope of resolution.

"This is none of our concern." I closed the book with one swift motion. "It's nothing more than a message from the past."

"What you are talking about, Alice?" Emery demanded. "That's precisely the reason it needs our attention! Perhaps the message is connected to the Lennox clan. You cannot dismiss it with insignificance."

"I have done no such thing," I snapped. "These past few weeks have granted me the proper time to muse over matters of the heart. I never asked for the role I have been given, really, and I would like to spend a few more days in peace."

"Heroines are not given the privilege to choose," said Emery. "You have mistaken selfishness for self-care, and you are wise enough to know the difference."

My sister's words pricked with guilt. She stared back for a few moments, reading the wounds that scarred my expression. As always, she recognized the mask that shielded my emotions.

"Do not be ashamed of fear," said Emery. "Rather, fear the inability to overcome it. You are strong, and courage has the power to guide you in the proper direction."

I placed the book inside an open trunk and dared to meet the eyes of my sister. Oceans of blue, irreplaceable blue. Behind her soft character, the strength of armor was found. As I sighed with defeat, a smile spread across her face.

CHAPTER FIVE

"Rise, and shine like the morning star!" Mother's voice pierced through the darkness of my dreams. The previous night had passed with slow strides, and the morning arrived with a sudden start.

"Oh, what time is it?" I groaned.

"Eight o'clock, dear one," she replied in a voice that reminded me of a song. "Your father has prepared the horses, and we are loading the trunks into the carriage."

My eyes shot open. Golden light trickled through windows, sweeping across the hardwood floor. I leaped out of bed. A single riding gown waited behind the door of the otherwise empty wardrobe. The threaded fabric and silver clasps contrasted the hues of my red curls.

"Breakfast is waiting in the kitchen," Mother told me. "You've no time to dilly-dally!"

I nodded in silence as she retreated from the chamber. After lifting the nightgown over my head, I released my hair from a tangled braid. The typical attire of Aisling required more attention than the blouses and jeans of the world beyond the portal. Medieval shifts and uncomfortable corsets formed layers under the average gown. Nevertheless, admiration for such fashion never seemed to fade.

I folded the ivory nightgown and glanced back at the reflection in the mirror. My leather boots gleamed against the faint light of morning. Freckles masked the circles around my tired eyes, and not a trace of makeup covered my skin. As I stood before the looking glass, a smile spread across my lips. For the first time in forever, the beauty of that countenance was not hidden from my eyes. Confidence seeped through my veins like flames that whispered words of courage.

As I stepped through the chamber door, those elements of comfort remained behind me. The corridors were empty, and the only sound could be traced into the distance. I swayed on my feet for a moment, discerning the dreams that dwelled in the corners of my heart. My eyes closed to welcome hopeful visions of the future.

"Alice!" A shout of excitement sounded from the entrance hall.

I opened my eyes.

"I'm coming!" I replied.

The vast unknown awaited me.

I hurried to the end of the corridor and turned to glance at the kindred portraits displayed on the walls.

My grandmother greeted me with bright hair and pale eyes. She was younger than the wise woman known to me. Her face was smooth and girlish, reflecting her immortal spirit.

Her memory gave me renewed strength.

As I descended the stairwell, colorful reflections danced across the wood. A group of familiar voices spoke beyond the open doorway, where my father stood with a brown-haired couple. A winged girl waited beside one of the carriage horses, patting his neck as she whistled a tune.

"Kade!" I exclaimed before running down the final steps. "What are you doing here?"

"Good morning," my friend spoke with a mischievous smile. "On our way to the castle, my brother convinced the coachman to stop at Macnas Manor. He said a few extra hands would be helpful to the Hanley clan, but it seems your father has managed to load the carriage. At present, our parents are engrossed in conversation."

"Well, no matter!" I laughed at the lazy roll of her eyes. "I would never pass an opportunity to speak with you. Where has your brother wandered?"

"Ah, Ronan," said Kade. Her voice picked up a hint of amusement. "He's helping your mother in the kitchen. I suppose you would rather converse with him."

"Oh, nonsense!" I exclaimed. "You are looking to stir trouble."

The dark-haired girl did not speak another word, while a childish grin flashed across her cheeks. A swirl of lavender fabric swept around her legs, like a breeze

41

in the final days of autumn. She turned to step through the front door as though it were the entrance to her own abode.

"Macnas Manor never fails to leave me enchanted," Kade murmured. "It's a strange place, in my opinion. The air seems to hold the finest traces of Gifted magic, and few homes are blessed with such an essence."

"My father would be thrilled to hear such a statement," I responded as we entered the kitchen.

My mother and sister were seated behind the counter, conversing in tones of delight. An abundance of herbs rested before them, organized in neat piles. The fragrance of dried lavender and chamomile rushed over me, along with the perfume of unknown spices. A few glass jars waited to preserve the blends of tea.

"There you are!" said Emery. A swift sigh escaped her lungs, and her attention flashed over my shoulders. "We've been waiting for you."

"Good morning, Alice," a voice spoke from behind me. I did not need to turn and greet the speaker, for his tone was too familiar to mistake. In the silence that replaced his words, a familiar smile painted in my mind. Such a masterpiece beckoned to be compared until I turned to the original work. It was freckled and imperfect, complete with a single dimple, but it touched my soul with pure rapture.

"Hello, Ronan," I regarded my friend with a gentle nod. "I did not expect to see your family at this hour of the morning! Kade tells me your horses are bound for the castle."

"Well, I'm always pleased to be entertained," said Ronan. "The Academy for Gifted Youth calls my name, but it would never stop me from visiting this house. After all, it rests beside the road to the moorlands."

"We are preparing to leave as well," my mother spoke with a sigh. "It will be good to have company on the journey." After filling the final jar of tea leaves, she dusted off her apron and tossed it over the chair. Her brown eyes sparkled, while the remaining perfume began to dissipate.

After a few moments, the gathering returned to the outdoors. Soft grass and bright light replaced the creaking floorboards and ancient walls. Solitude was found in both places, but the sounds of nature provided a proper sanctuary for the soul.

After waving his hands with impatience, my father leaped for the reins of his carriage. He pulled a watch out of his pocket to examine the time. "My dear girls," he called, "there is not a single moment to waste!"

I laughed before bidding farewell to my friends. Whistling songbirds swept through the morning air, like careful reminders of the occasion. I glanced back at the old house that stood beside the path. Behind those stone walls, hidden libraries, passages, and memories dwelled. They spoke in the tone of a faint whisper, urging me to move forward with strength.

❦❦❦

Gnarled oak trees moved behind the window in a haze of green and gold. I stared through the glass for several minutes, attempting to catch sight of the castle in the distance. My mind raced with impatience, while the horses moved through the glistening woods.

Mother was focused on the thick novel in her hands. She traced a finger across the lines of ink as though the words promised comfort in times of distress. Her pale brow furrowed in a thoughtful expression, which told me that she was not focused on the tale of fiction. It wasn't difficult to imagine the troubles that burdened her mind. After the recent turn of events, her twin daughters moved toward an unknown fate. She wanted to hide us in a tall tower, away from the strange mysteries, dark creatures, and growing dangers of the realm. She wanted to bring us back to the simple days of childhood.

My father's voice drifted through the open window, sharing the words of an old folksong. Despite the coaches that trailed behind us, the man continued to sing with jubilation. It was quite difficult to read his emotions, for he never revealed more than a hint. Every now and then, the ballad was interrupted as he spoke to the pair of horses. His voice was rather tired, and each word brimmed with concern.

As we approached the final curve in the road, Emery leaned forward to whisper against my ear. She had inherited the face of our father—gentle, pale, and indecipherable. "Your hair is sparking again," she noticed.

I replied with a careless shrug.

The castle appeared in full view as we crossed the forest border. It was a magnificent sight. A line of coaches and mounted riders trailed away from the entrance. The courtyard bloomed with the fading shades of summer, and wild vines climbed over the stone walls.

Gifted students dashed across the grounds, enveloped in laughter. The breeze carried delightful conversations of reunion. A warm essence floated around the scene, weaving between horses and shouts of banter. It was the muse of prose and poetry.

As the carriage approached the castle steps, silence settled over the crowd. All eyes turned to look in our direction. The stares did not burn with disapproval; rather, the Gifted people greeted us with admiration.

"They're watching," I whispered.

I was not fond of the attention. Flames began to climb over my ginger curls. The curtained windows allowed me to hide from the curiosity of the other students.

"Listen," Emery spoke in a gentle tone. "Can you hear the music?" Her voice pulled me away from the gathering crowd, like a wisp of light in the darkness. I listened for the sound of music, but there was nothing to be heard—not a single tune of the fiddle or melody of the piano.

My sister watched me with a careful expression, holding one finger against her lips. She closed her eyes, and after a moment, I followed her example. The voices began to fade as the songs of sparrows shifted into focus. I heard the ballad of unknown insects, which scurried across the forest floor. I listened to the whisper of the wind, which arrived from the northern mountains. Flickering flames appeared in the castle windows, illuminating the chandeliers of the entrance hall. The light seemed to beckon me with outstretched arms.

As my father opened the door of the coach, there was nowhere else to hide. I glanced around for a moment before accepting his outstretched hand. It did not take long for me to realize the stares of classmates were nothing more than an illusion that covered the smiles.

"Well then," a voice called from the assemblage. "If it isn't the Hanley sisters!"

"Indeed," I replied as a familiar figure stepped into the open. "Though one might be more astonished by the mere presence of himself!"

Fionn laughed before running a hand though his tow-colored hair. It was no longer tied back with a piece of twine, as his father had set about to cut it short. The strands were fair and less tangled than before. In my opinion, he suited the role of a gentleman. As my sister stepped out of the carriage, his blue gaze dropped with hesitation.

A trumpet sounded beside the open doors, calling all students to enter the castle. The crowd began to disperse before my sister had a chance to meet the eyes of our friend. Father unloaded the trunks and handed them off to a group of men. He turned to look at us with an unreadable expression.

"My dear girls," he said, "your father is a sentimental man."

"And that is one of the many reasons I love him so," said Emery. After a moment, she placed two fingers beside the corners of his mouth, attempting to reverse the frown in his expression. Our father chuckled before gathering her in his arms.

"Remember—you are closer now than ever before," I reminded him. "And you have raised a pair of strong women."

Before taking the reins, he turned his attention to me. "Alice," he said, "there was a time when I told you to have courage. But now, I tell you to have faith." He kissed my forehead before climbing into his seat on the coach.

My mother closed her novel and placed it to the side. As she stroked her hand across my cheek, her brown eyes flooded with pride and sorrow. "*Grá mo chroí*," she whispered, calling me the love of her heart. "You are a bright star in the valley of darkness. Shine your light into the shadows."

I wrapped my arms around her shoulders and pulled her close. The corners of her eyes crinkled into a smile of warmth. As I rested my chin on her shoulder, the scent of fresh flowers swept over me. It reminded me of the meadows behind the castle, the fields that welcomed me home. The trumpet sounded for the second time before I stepped through the castle doors.

An opal chandelier floated high above our heads. Suspended in the air, it almost seemed weightless. Delicate flames danced behind the jewels, which reflected the colors of the afternoon light.

Emery stood beside my right shoulder, prepared to face the crowd of people. Her fingers were clothed in lace, and her toes were suited in leather boots. Her blonde hair was pulled back with a single ribbon of black velvet. She was the epitome of feminine fortitude.

47

"There you are!" a green-eyed girl exclaimed from the gathering that poured through the entrance hall. She pushed against fellow students before stepping away from the crowd. The sunlight shifted to shine upon her face.

"Juniper!" I greeted her.

"I have been searching for you," she addressed both of us. "Fionn and Ariadne are seated in the dining hall. The ceremony will begin soon—follow me."

A pair of armored knights stood beside the doorway. Despite their fierce expressions, the men were merely assigned to open the entrance as needed. Their attire was not typical of the Guardians of Aisling, and their eyes were not so gentle. The knights stared beyond my shoulders, as if they did not recognize one of the Hanley sisters. Their silver swords sparkled with the reflections of the crowd.

A shiver of discomfort swept over my arms.

This matter seemed to fade as I stepped into the dining hall. The tables spread out in several rows, adorned with fresh linen and wildflowers. Children dashed across the floor, and teenagers laughed beside open windows. Gifted magic surrounded me. Some powers were visible, while others traced to the mind. White-and-blue banners swayed with the breeze that was summoned by the hands of a friend.

"Welcome back," Ariadne greeted us.

The petite girl squeezed through the crowd of people. All thoughts of composure and indifference abandoned, she clapped her hands in merriment. Her short hair was braided in a delicate fashion, which bounced as she strode across the floor. "Of course, it has only been a week, but it seems like ages have passed!"

With a graceful wave of her hands, Ariadne led the way to the proper table. The train of her gown followed with patience, while the hushed wind gathered around her ankles.

"Do you see the headmistress?" Emery gestured toward the long table of professors.

Zara Hawthorne was seated in the middle, engrossed in conversation with Sir Barrington. Her dark hair and fair skin stood out, like a raven in the snow. She was regal, collected, and everything a leader ought to be. Even so, her loyalties were not defined. It was difficult to trust the woman who stood in silence at Castle Moss.

CHAPTER SIX

When evening settled over the realm, there was much to think about. I stood alone in the library, where the scent of old books lingered between shelves. A smile of contentment spread across my lips, as the love of literature promised to remain with me.

A tale of folklore opened in my hands. Faded illustrations adored pages of the ancient work. Each word told the tale of the maiden whom the realm was named after.

Aislinn was the first child to discover her Gift, as she befriended the elements of earth, water, wind, and fire. She lived in a far-off land, nestled between frozen mountains. Several villagers were frightened of her powers, and the ruler of the distant isle sent her into exile. She drifted across the blue ocean, until her lone rowboat was swallowed by the waves. Unable to swim, she fell under the deep water, closing her eyes against salt and tears.

A merman discovered the girl in a bed of coral, and he pitied her face of innocence. He breathed life into her lungs and carried her through the portal to this realm. She opened her eyes to the silver shores, and the name of magic slipped from her mouth. She lived there for many years, raised by the faeries who dwelled in the moorlands. As the days passed, a trace of loneliness entered her heart, and it grew like the wildflowers in the fields. She longed to speak with a kindred spirit, to see the face of a human being. The creatures of the realm tried to cure her sorrow with laughter and tonics, but the results did not last for long.

One morning, in the fog of dawn, a man appeared in the birch forest. He stumbled across the maiden as she wept beside the stream. An old voice spoke to him, revealing the tale of the Gifted woman. As he greeted her eyes, the maiden smiled with the knowledge that she was not alone in the kingdom.

Marking my page in the middle of the chapter, I turned my attention to the setting sun. A neat collection of novels was stacked against the windowsill. Shadows collected around the bindings, which shielded tales of mischief and magic. A golden veil covered the castle walls, and danced between trees in the distance.

My gaze caught on a sudden flash of red. A small fox waited near the edge of the woodland. His tail flicked with the sort of irritation that was characteristic of an impatient man. The creature paced through the grass, with eyes fixed sharply on the tower of Lancaster Hall.

Killian.

I hurried back through the rows and down the spiraled stairwell, leaving the world of fiction behind. Students and professors turned to watch me rush through the crowded corridors. I did not care enough to hear their remarks. A trail of wonder and ember sparks followed in my footsteps.

A pair of knights waited in the entrance hall. Their expressions were stern and full of suspicion, but there was not a single question to be asked. They exchanged a brief glance before opening the doors in front of me. I walked forward with confident strides, and dared not to meet their eyes.

The wind greeted me with a gentle kiss, which whispered in words of conversation. I closed my eyes and dared to listen. It was nothing like the song of nature, for the blissful breeze was masked by the harsh tones it carried.

Curiosity led me to the edge of the courtyard. Between stone walls and flowering heather, a dark-haired girl stood beside her father. Her cheeks were damp with tears, but her gaze was cold and careless. A white flower twirled between her fingers, unable to escape from the electric snare. She did not take notice of my presence, as thick vines shielded my red hair.

A warning rushed through my core, stirring the fire in my veins. It told me to retreat, run, and hide, but there was no sense in such action.

"You are a disappointment, Cleona," the man spoke to his daughter. His words struck me with account for a prick of pity. "Your powers have no place in this realm."

"You seemed to think otherwise when you learned the truth about the Hanley sisters," Cleo sneered. "As I recall, you begged me to ruin their chance of success."

The feeling of compassion faded.

"And you failed," Sir Lennox snapped.

"On account of her Guardian!" Cleo recoiled. "Without his interference, that ginger witch would have been buried in the ground."

"You underestimate her," Sir Lennox replied. "Despite her Gift, one mustn't deny her abilities. She will outmatch you in every class of strength."

The girl remained silent. Silver light flashed across her fingertips, which held the flower between electric waves. A deep anger burned in her eyes, which reflected nothing more than her father's displeasure.

"Spying, are you?"

Killian appeared beside the castle wall. His mouth curled in a mischievous smile, which revealed two lines of teeth. He possessed the strength of both man and canine, and he knew of the proper time to use it.

"I was looking for you," I whispered.

"Of course," said Killian. "Although, you appear rather distracted from the task."

I held one finger against my lips. My eyes flicked toward the courtyard. The little fox looked at me with a stern expression. His nose twitched for a moment before he recognized the scent of the Lennox clan. I watched as his muzzle curled with unfamiliar aggression.

"Follow me," Killian ordered, before trotting back down the path.

After one last glance into the courtyard, I turned to follow the creature. The echoes of conversation faded away like wisps of smoke in the night.

"Where are we going?" I inquired. "I thought you would care enough to listen."

"Your safety is my greatest concern," said Killian. "Lachlan waits to speak about matters of true importance."

"What do you consider a matter of true importance?" I demanded. "The Lennox clan continues to threaten the Four Elementals. Such revenge does not fight with ease. You should have listened to their words of hatred. I am nothing more than an obstacle that must be pushed down."

"No, Alice," said Killian. "You are a flame that can never be extinguished."

The ginger fox led me through a row of heather, which passed a gathering of young students. Voices of innocence and laughter flowed between the branches, while leaves tickled my nose with persistence. The children startled as a sneeze overwhelmed my senses. Their tones of delight transformed into whispers of the haunted woods. I gasped and covered my mouth as the group returned to the castle.

The fox rolled his eyes and continued onward. We reached the edge of the Night Oak Forest, where sunlight replaced shadows. A stream rushed through the tree roots, in search of the perfect place to fall.

Killian stopped between the gnarled oaks, which towered far above our heads. After a long silence, the fox released a shrill howl that was sure to frighten the eldest students. His ears perked forward in attention.

"What are you doing?" I demanded.

"*Dún do bhéal!*" Killian snapped. His paws were damp with dewdrops, but his gaze burned through the forest.

The surrounding trees were covered in layers of moss, which climbed over the grooves and knots in the bark. I walked forward on careful strides. My right hand reached out to touch an unusual patch of lichen.

"Best keep those hands to yourself, lass," a strong voice spoke. "I'd prefer to keep the beard on my chin."

I gasped as a layer of bark moved away from the tree. A plump man held it forward like a shield. His eyes were bright and full of humor. His leather armor suggested the title of a Guardian of Aisling. The forest breathed a light-hearted sigh, as a band of warriors stepped forward to meet us.

"We have been waiting for you," said Lachlan.

I turned to greet the familiar man. His hair was rugged and seemed to lack the care given to his bow and arrows. A deep crease was settled between his eyebrows.

"Your entrance is worthy of applause," I remarked, "but I do not understand the need for such theatrics."

"This meeting must be discreet," said Lachlan. "The Guardians of Aisling act against the orders of Sir Bastian Amulet."

"What do you mean?" I questioned.

Lachlan remained silent and turned his head to glance at Killian. Their inaudible conversation continued for a moment before the fox sighed.

"The Order of Birch believes the Elementals have served their purpose," said Killian. "The Creatures of the Night Oak Forest have been vanquished, and the Siren Sisters have been destroyed. The prophecy of the headmistress is complete."

"You must act with care," Lachlan continued. "I have reason to believe the Order of Birch has been infiltrated. Amulet has assigned a group of knights to the castles. His attitudes have changed toward the Guardians, as the views of his comrades impose upon his foolish mind."

"He is nothing more than a spineless scoundrel!" one of the female warriors shouted.

The others huffed and nodded in agreement. Betrayal and resentment were written in the dirt across their faces. "Mark my words," added one of the men. "A battle looms on the horizon."

"You must know something I do not." I searched their eyes for an answer, but such colors of emotion did not speak to me.

"You have been thrust into a world that existed long before your own life," said Lachlan. "But somehow, you are here to mend the broken pieces."

CHAPTER SEVEN

As dawn peeked through the castle windows, anticipation danced within me. It was the first day of classes, and there was much to think about. Light poured through the glass, casting beams across the dusted floors. It greeted me with a gentle kiss, a reminder that darkness falls short of daylight.

"Alice," a voice called from across the room. "Are you awake?" It was the silvery and unmistakable tone of my sister.

"Yes," I replied.

"Lovely," Emery whispered.

Our brief exchange was followed by the hushed sound of bare feet on the hardwood floor. As I opened my eyes, the fair-haired girl crouched beside my bed. Her blue eyes brimmed with anxious wonder.

"You must tell me about your meeting with Killian," said Emery. "There is no place for secrets in sisterhood."

"What are you talking about?" I questioned, rubbing the sleep away from my eyes.

"Last night," she responded. "I watched you follow him to the edge of the forest."

I sighed after a long moment, allowing the silence to settle between us. A haze of confusion surrounded my interaction with the Guardians of Aisling. The warriors did not care to share details, but fear tainted their words. Each one spoke an ominous warning.

"We are mere girls," I murmured, "with the weight of the realm on our shoulders."

Emery huffed before pinching my wrist with a touch of frost. I jumped in surprise. Her brows furrowed in frustration.

"Don't be stupid," she said. "Though we are the fair ones, women are not to be trifled with! A precious strength lives within our souls, and it will guide us through the battlefield."

We stared at each other for a long time, until the clouds parted to reveal cerulean skies. Daylight tugged at my sleeves. I slipped out of bed to sit on the floor beside my sister. A swirl of ice encircled her toes while she rested her chin upon her knees.

"We are not alone," said Emery. "While few people stand against us, many stand with us."

A creak of the wood turned my attention to the pair of girls in the center of the chamber. Juniper ran her fingers through a long braid, while Ariadne stared back in silence.

I glanced into their eyes with hesitation. Our friendship was stronger than the threats of a thousand forces. Together, our powers connected to the vital elements of nature, and there was hope to be found in the whole of creation.

"Oh, Alice," said Ariadne. "You seem to forget you are a fair maiden, warrior, and queen."

"So are you." I smiled. "All of you, really!"

"No matter what happens, until the very end," said Juniper, "we shall always be the best of friends. Never forget that."

When time beckoned students to class, the halls rang with the ballad of the bell tower. Each clang echoed through my mind, speaking the promise of new beginnings. I was crowned in jewels of renewed courage. A river of conversation flowed through the corridors. A young knight walked beside the tapestries, snuffing the lanterns perched on the walls. The flames transformed into white smoke, which danced like spirits of the night.

I wandered down the stone passages, until an open door revealed the proper classroom. Unmarked by numbers, the entrance was adorned with a sign that indicated the name of the professor. Each letter gleamed in the sunlight, while the scent of fresh chalk and paper lingered in the air. A small group of students was seated on the floor, engrossed in the latest gossip. I glanced around for a moment before leaning against the wall.

"Oh, poor lamb," a voice spoke from the shadowed corner. "You are lost without those frivolous friends."

Ebony eyes peered through the patch of darkness. Cleona stepped forward, followed by a trail of scarlet fabric. Her lips curled into a sneer, while her eyes fixed on me. The other students glanced over their shoulders with suspicion. Although Cleona was not well-admired, several girls followed her with the persistence of a shadow. Their companionship wavered with the fears of cowards. Such foolish hearts search for a dangerous form of acceptance.

Do not respond, Alice. It isn't worth the effort.

"The entire realm believes you are a heroine," Cleo scorned. "Then again, half the people are vacuous."

A fire burned in my veins, begging for the freedom to leap forward. It dared to damage, to make her regret words of little worth. A song whispered in the depths of the chaos; it spoke in the language of my soul. Beneath the music, there was a connection to be found.

"Oh, Lennox." I scoffed. "You are wasting precious time. The Gifted are well aware of the mysteries that surround your clan, and it would not be improper to assume their displeasure. Perhaps you should find a victim who cares to acknowledge hollow remarks."

Cleo remained silent as the chamber filled with students. Her heart was consumed by the ashes of anger. Even so, there was a trace of fear in her eyes. Sparks of electricity traveled across her fingertips, raising the hair on my arms. Her gaze narrowed as she glanced behind me.

"Good morning, ladies," said Oliver. "I hope you have prepared for the first lesson of the semester."

Several moments passed before the tall man stood beside me. A pair of round spectacles balanced on the tip of his nose, while his eyes peered down with hesitation. He placed a hand on my shoulder in a protective manner.

Cleona stalked off without response. After all, she possessed little strength in a castle of candlelight.

"Your timing is impeccable," I greeted the man.

"Envy creeps under her skin," Oliver observed with a distant stare. His lips turned into a slight frown. "It paints in hues of red and gold."

The young professor stood there for a minute, attracting the attention of curious students. In the midst of conversation, his mind traveled through the emotions of others. He felt the delight of children and heartbreak of lovers.

"Well then," Oliver proclaimed, after shifting back into focus. He proceeded to stride across the room and work through the eternal list of rules. "During this fine hour, students shall learn about the Gifts of Aisling. This includes connection, usage, and classification. While this classroom serves as shelter from the elements, students will be expected to gather in the meadows. Stone walls do not accommodate for the occasional explosion.

"Students will learn the value of their abilities through self-defense," he continued. "Particular lessons require more than one professor; therefore, do not be alarmed by the sight of Sir Barrington. To be honest, his appearance is worse than his bite."

A trickle of laughter followed this statement.

"Follow me, children." Oliver waved his hands before marching through the doorway. His leather shoes tapped across the marble. There was not a single person in the corridor, and all of the classrooms appeared to be empty.

61

As we reached the stairwell, shades of emerald peeked through open doors.

Students wandered through the forests, fields, and flowering courtyard. Some trailed after professors, while others were guided by nothing more than the imagination.

"What do you hear?" Oliver asked as the class gathered under the shade of a willow tree.

There was a moment of silence before one student replied. "Nothing."

"The breath of nature." Oliver smiled as his chest expanded.

A swift wind swept away from the forest and over the moorlands. It carried the whispers of autumn, which chilled the surface of my skin. Wildflowers cowered in the remaining warmth of the summer sun. Insects hushed their cheerful chorus, as sparrows glided along the breeze.

"As the semester moves forward, this class will provide valuable relationships with your peers, talents, and surroundings," said Oliver. "Before such tasks can be achieved, a deep connection must form between the Gift and the Gifted."

CHAPTER EIGHT

A single day passed before I stood on the path of the Night Oak Forest. Emery paced the tree line with graceful strides and tentative glances. I leaned against one of the moss-covered trees, caught in conversation with Ariadne Moss. A pair of nightingales perched to observe our interaction.

When the birds dared to sing, my eyes lifted to the sight of Juniper Stone. The wild girl stumbled into the woodland, burdened by the mere thought of tardiness. A light basket slung around her left arm.

"You're late," said Ariadne, as though she were required to state the obvious.

"I'm *aware*." Juniper sighed. "You really must forgive me! Sir Barrington intercepted me on the way out of the castle. He inquired about a piece of my writing from last year, wondering about the possibility of sharing it with first-year students."

"Very well!" Emery cheered.

"Of course," said Ariadne, attempting to hide her dry sense of humor. "Not all of us can be so talented in academia."

Without much delay, we passed through the deep woods. There was much to muse over in the land that once sheltered invisible beasts. Soft earth cushioned the sound of our steps, which sauntered in a scrupulous manner. Knotted trees sheltered creatures of the wide-eyed sort.

"Do you suppose they feel the loss of the beasts?" Emery gestured to an unusual pair of hares.

"Perhaps," said Ariadne. "Although I doubt there was an hour of mourning."

Beside the woodland trail, a cluster of rosebushes bloomed in sunlight. My attention focused on the rustle of branches. A flash of white appeared behind the leaves, followed by the distinct flutter of wings. A pair of round eyes blinked between thorns.

"Did you see that?" I halted on the path.

"Just ignore it." Ariadne sighed. "It wouldn't be the first creature to hunt in the afternoon."

As we neared the edge of a clear stream, the sound of wings approached once more. I glanced back to see an owl perched in the branches of a large tree. It appeared to be following us.

"We are being watched," Juniper observed.

Shrugging with lack of suspicion, no one stopped to speak with the bird. His sharp talons and white feathers gleamed in the dappled light. As we moved forward, he did not care enough to follow, but his stare burned through the back of my neck. Perhaps he was a Guardian, assigned to watch over us. A trickle of doubt entered my mind, for there was not a tint of gold in his eyes. Even so, the owl was aware of his quest, which did not seem to involve the hunt of toads.

The brook widened as a small bridge reached over the water. Pieces of driftwood combined with fine boards, in order to create a proper path over the stream. I gazed down at the gaps between the wood. Reflections danced across the water, mimicking the hues of my hair. As I stepped toward the other side, a pair of eyes peered through the final crevice, accompanied by a twitching nose.

A sudden scream escaped from me.

"What in all of Aisling?" Emery breathed.

"Oh, look!" said Juniper, admiring the round creature that crawled out from under the bridge. The strange thing was coated in a thick head of dandelion seeds. The white-and-yellow fuzz surrounded his head, like the mane of an adult lion. His nose pointed out like that of a hedgehog, while his ears rounded like those of a bear cub. A pair of bright eyes protruded from his face, unwilling to blink for the fear of predators. Despite his peculiar appearance, the creature was rather adorable.

"It's nothing more than a wee tarawisp!" Ariadne laughed.

"Excuse me?"

"Never fear," said Juniper. "Tarawisps are known to be quite affectionate creatures. They often sleep in forgotten teacups in the back of the cupboard. Gypsies sell breeding pairs at the summer market, but this one appears to be wild."

Juniper scooped the tarawisp into her hands and placed him on her freckled shoulder. Her expression did not contain a trace of concern. "I shall call him Peb," she hummed.

"Something is wrong," Emery said. She stood beside the rail of the bridge, focused on the stream that rushed underneath. "The water is disturbed and refuses to speak with me."

Ariadne glanced around with a raised eyebrow. The breeze carried whispers to her ears, messages only she could understand. With a finger held against her lips, she listened with careful attention. Her gaze flicked toward the large oak that stood down the path. Its deep roots traveled underground, like veins under the skin. Twisted branches climbed into the canopy, where a small bear looked down with interest.

"Clara," Ariadne murmured.

The wind picked up a sweep of ivory fabric, which flowed from the other side of the tree. After a long moment, the young girl appeared, and the bear scurried down to stand at her side. A delicate tiara crowned her head of curls. She greeted us with a simple nod and flash of opal eyes.

"Clara," I spoke to the child. "What brings you to the Night Oak Forest?"

"Are you following us?" Ariadne demanded.

"I've been searching for you," the girl replied in a cool tone. Her dress was torn and stained with grass, and her expression revealed little of her emotions.

"Is something wrong?" Emery asked.

"Yes," said Clara. "For one, you are never easy to find. Since your last visit to the birch territories, there has been much activity in the forest. The trails are congested with coaches, and the animals are anxious. I've spoken to the Guardians about the matter, and the archers blame the Order of Birch. I do not wish to alarm you, but there are whispers in the woods. Many creatures are concerned for the protection of the Four Elementals."

Emery turned to glance at me. Her blue eyes pleaded for answers to unspoken questions.

"I do not wish to speak words of treason," Clara continued. "Nevertheless, you must know the truth. I have learned about the sinister spirit that lurks in Castle Moss. Such darkness floats through open windows and enters the treetops. It infects the Order of Birch and penetrates through the light of the forest. Soon enough, the headmistress will stand alone in a battle against the convictions of the Lennox clan."

"I have reason to doubt her allegiance," I replied, reeling over the powerful voice of the young queen.

"If so, you must be unaware of her struggle," said Clara. "Sir Lennox has found a place in the Order of Birch, and his influence looms over the reign of Amulet. So long as he remains, there is a threat against the status of the headmistress. She stands for the protection and true value of all, while the Lennox clan fights for the hierarchy and classification of the Gifted."

"Pity arrives at the strangest moments," Juniper murmured. "Sir Lennox has a cold heart, devoid of mercy and compassion. The loss of his wife was tragic, and his faith was not strong enough to lead him through the fog. His daughter was foolish to follow in his footsteps."

"Listen to my warning," Clara insisted. "You are the last hope of the realm."

Without another word, the little girl climbed onto the back of the largest bear. She tucked her fingers through his fur and spurred him forward with her heels. Lazy strides carried her into the distance. I watched in silence as she disappeared between the scattered trees. The stream promised to lead them back to the land of white birches.

"Alice?" My sister's voice broke through the essence of the unknown. "Did you hear me, Alice?

"What?"

As the group continued to walk down the path, Emery turned to look at me. Oceans danced behind her eyes. Frost formed on her cheekbones, catching the sunlight in fleeting glimmers. "A dark ghost looms before us, and it does not dwell in the Night Oak Forest," said Emery. "The memories of Wolfgang Gregory have faded with time, but his beliefs dare to return with renewed influence."

"Secrets are destined to be revealed," Juniper added. "Sir Lennox was surely involved in the disappearance of the Lost Dreamer. Orinthia's notes have attempted to confirm this suspicion. The truth will open the eyes of the Gifted people."

"Unless someone can take us back in time, there is no way to identify the connection," said Ariadne.

"There is *someone*," Juniper responded.

"Who?"

"Lydia Ludwig," said Juniper. "She has the power to read visions from the past. I have seen her take childhood memories from a lock of my mother's hair. She says these visions can be found in many things. Perhaps she can help us."

"Very well!" said Emery. "What are we waiting for?"

"Lydia is a tight-lipped woman. She doesn't care to use her Gift often," said Juniper. "It is considered strange and powerful, and she fears the backlash of the Lennox clan."

"We will need to convince her," said Ariadne.

As we rounded the final bend of the trail, the voices of villagers moved between trees. Dark shadows and ridges made way for stone cottages and storefronts. A distant melody lulled the sound of horseshoes trotting down the roads. In the heart of town, the buildings hugged a maze of narrow sidewalks. Unfamiliar flowers lined the shutters of every home, where ladies poured hydration from buckets. Ancient traces of magic lingered in the air, sweeping through archways and open windows.

Strangers turned to watch as we strolled through the village of Willowcrest. Shopkeepers paused in conversation with customers, captivated by our presence. Word traveled like a wildfire in the realm of Aisling, and the news of Fionn's return spanned far beyond the shores of Innis. An image of our faces latched onto the tale of the forgotten child.

"They are staring at us," Ariadne grumbled. "Why must they always stare at us?"

"The villagers believe in heroism," Juniper replied. "For now, we are the subjects of rumors and printed papers. Be grateful you aren't standing in the shoes of the Lost Dreamer."

"Fionn doesn't seem to mind the attention." Emery sighed. "Rather, he is concerned about catching up with his peers. He dozed off in class this morning, and Sir Barrington cuffed him over the head. His excessive hours of study have received little empathy from the professors."

The others paid little attention to my sister's ramblings. Juniper's tarawisp hid in her wild mane, sniffing the white flowers that rested behind her ears. Petals fell like snowflakes on the cobblestone street, but the boughs never seemed to run out of blossoms. As we entered a small bakery, the scent of warm pastries filled my lungs. The tarawisp peeked between tangled curls, drooling over cinnamon and buttercream frosting.

"Don't you dare, Peb!" Ariadne warned. "Such an amount of sugar would result in terrible digestion."

"Oh, never mind!" Juniper laughed, sneaking the creature a crumb from the sample dish.

With a childish twinkle in her eyes, the girl requested a box of lionberry tarts. The baker was an elderly woman with thick braids and pink ribbons. As a matter of fact, she was never seen in attire that did not possess a shade of pink. Even her spectacles were framed in the color, which complimented the stain of blush on her cheeks. Without a word, she exchanged the pastries for a handful of silver coins.

We studied beside the rosebushes that bloomed on the edge of the forest. Enchanted creatures and unusual powers poured into the corners of my imagination. My fingers trailed over the textbooks that attempted to make a connection with the fire in my veins. Children dashed through the fields that surrounded the village. Afternoon faded into the evening, until I found myself in the castle once more.

CHAPTER NINE

The next few weeks passed with anticipation. September drew to a close, along with the final trace of summer. A crisp autumn wind swept over the castle grounds. Assignments littered the floors of Lancaster Hall, while students studied in the shadows of bookshelves. Warm tea accompanied professors in the classrooms and open fields, and the birch forest burned in the ashes of golden foliage. Cloaks and wool sweaters clothed the Gifted students. Time remained before the first snowfall of winter, which never continued for more than a single month.

The headmistress did not demand written tests from the students; rather, she expected the improvement of control—a strengthened bond between the Gift and the Gifted.

Although powers are individual, each manifests in a similar form, and one learns from the talents of another. I learned this truth from my mother, but I did not understand until further studies detailed the link between heart and soul. The notion was an answer to childhood prayers. The previous year gave me confidence to find this connection, and time bestowed a name upon it.

I looked forward to the final class of the evening, when Oliver gathered his students in those fields behind the castle. The youthful professor instructed with spirit, unlike the scrupulous teachings of others. On the final day of the month, Oliver led his class to a platform on the edge of the woodland. A group of younger students spied behind the trunk of an old sycamore.

"I've heard of this place," Emery remarked.

"Ah, yes!" said Oliver. "Welcome to the training grounds. Legend tells us this stage was built on the site of the final battle between Silas Casper and Wolfgang Gregory. True evidence was never discovered, though some claim the tree fungus to be scars of Wolfgang's decay. As I mentioned weeks ago, the study of Gifts includes the art of self-defense. For the rest of today's class, we shall focus on this subject."

"It's more than true," Cleo whispered in the ears of her friends. "I hope you are prepared—one never cares to fight a weakling."

After several minutes, the class divided into pairs. I reached for the hand of my sister, only to find her beside

Fionn. She shrugged with a nonchalant expression, gesturing toward the remaining students. As I turned in a careful circle, the number of gentle faces diminished. Few people dared to contend with burning flames—and electricity. My heart sank as the final option stood before me.

"Oh, how marvelous!" Cleona curled her lips in a twisted smile. Her teeth were like perfect pearls behind scarlet lips, prepared to bite an apple or drink the blood of a foe.

"There will come a time when you must fight for the honor and protection of those dearest to you." Oliver raised his voice over the hushed class. "Until then, you must learn to use your Gift as an advantage."

"So, what?" a red-haired lad demanded. "Do you expect us to fight on this ancient stage? I'm afraid the boards will break under such force."

"There is a difference between battle and civilized training," Oliver reassured. "For this assignment, students will face each other on the platform, only to experience the interaction of individual magic. Do not underestimate the power of the Gifted—there is grave danger in such a fault. As each of you learn the various methods of defense, exploration and instinct will be your guides."

A pair of unfamiliar students were first to face each other on the stage. The forest fell into silence as creatures turned their attention to the Gifted. When the peeping children refused to leave, the professor gestured for them to observe from the grass. With bouncing curls and bursts of laughter, the cherubs tumbled to the edge of the platform.

"Begin," said Oliver.

The female student closed her eyes with sudden force. In a matter of seconds, her surroundings transformed into a swirl of colors, which combined to form the abyss of space. Silver constellations appeared through the darkness, along with the light of the golden sun. Despite the marvels of such magic, my gaze did not divert from the girl in the center of the stage. There was something to learn from her eyelids, which fluttered with the strength of imagination.

With a clap of his hands, the other student shattered the illusion of his opponent. The girl opened her eyes to reveal a scowl of frustration, while the class released a synchronized gasp. A winged creature took flight and soared off the stage. It left nothing in place of the lad with golden eyes. After circling the trees, the griffin landed back on the platform.

"All right then!" Oliver shouted his praise. "Now, can this class describe the situation that unfolded between Astrid and Byrd?"

Emery raised her hand with hesitation. Her gaze wavered for a moment before the professor called her name. "Astrid was Gifted with illusion, which she utilized as a form of hypnosis. When Byrd noticed this, he used his transformation as a path to escape."

"Precisely, my dear!" Oliver exclaimed. "Lennox, Hanley—stand and deliver."

Cleo shot me a cold glare, as if her eyes were lethal daggers. All feelings of anticipation molded into a distinct sense of dread.

Calm down, Alice. You must control... control.

Ginger curls lifted with the flames that consumed my focus. As I stepped onto the platform, there was not a trace of control to grasp. Cleo's voice cut through the silence, like an iron blade on the battlefield. Discouragement was her greatest form of defense.

"Have you looked into a mirror, Alice?" she sneered. "You have no control over your Gift. In my opinion, it is a strong power gone to waste. The chaos started in flames, and it shall end in flames."

"Well then," I replied. "You waste far too many words on insult. That's enough for now."

With a flick of my wrist, flames leaped through the air, encircling me like a burning shield. Students staggered back from the stage, jaws dropped in stupefaction.

Cleo was barely visible through the dancing fire; nevertheless, she was there. Resentment and rage seeped through her expression. Her eyes flashed to the crowd for a moment, aware of the astonishment that stirred.

"Remember," Oliver warned, "this is nothing more than a good-natured training session."

A strange tension built around the interaction, while hair raised on my arms. Cleo stood quite still, holding her hands slightly apart. Contempt lingered behind her gaze, as though her chances of happiness were doomed by the mere existence of her opponent. Electric currents streamed toward her with a natural pull, and silver sparks jolted in the space between her hands. The waves continued to build until the power formed a fatal weapon.

"Why, Cleo?" I questioned. "What have I done to earn such malice? I don't understand."

"And you never will!" she cried.

A flash of lightning overwhelmed the skies, despite the shine of the cloudless morning. It seemed like a miracle from the heavens, although such light dared to blind. It did not strike me into the ground, but it touched down in the forest behind the platform. With a terrible groan and thunderous roar, something else flashed before my eyes.

A scream of terror escaped my sister, as she begged me to move forward. From the tone of her voice, a haunted image entered my mind. I tumbled across the wooden stage, pushed by the care of an unseen angel. Cleona's expression did not flicker as a blazing tree limb crashed down in my former place. As the gathering erupted into shouts of protest, the flames sought shelter from me. I whisked them away with a simple wave.

"Cleona Lennox," Oliver bellowed. "What have you done?" There was not a trace of forgiveness or sympathy in his voice; his usual tone of consideration was nowhere to be found.

The girl stumbled back for a moment as her gaze returned to focus. A touch of regret crossed her face before it vanished without a trace. "Do not place the blame on my shoulders!" Cleo responded. "The task is fulfilled, and I did not place a finger on her freckled skin."

"Your use of magic was an act of *violence*, not *defense*," said Oliver. "I do not care to learn about the strife that lingers between both of you. There is no excuse for such action, Lennox. One cannot help but notice the anger behind your eyes. It must be overturned."

Cleo did not apologize or plead for forgiveness; rather, she turned her back on the professor. She did not seek the acceptance of her peers, as she sought recognition in another. She would never be seen in the light she imagined. All thoughts of morality were stripped from her character, as her father did not accept anything of the sort.

A photograph shimmered in the locket around her neck. It contained the image of a woman with gentle eyes. Despite the pain of lost memories, her mother was never forgotten, not even amidst the darkness of the Lennox clan.

❦❧❧❦

As I stepped through the courtyard gate, three girls waited beside the gardens. My sister's voice traveled along the winds of autumn, which reminded me to lace the strings of my cloak. "*I have many dreams,*" Emery recited. "*Some are known to you, while others dwell inside my mind, like secrets of the blue.*" The words of poetry escaped her with an effortless sort of grace. An everlasting sea of dreams spread out across the evening skies. My mind was burdened with the weight of the unknown, but there was peace to be found in the careless rhythm of her voice.

The girls turned to look at me as the gate closed with a screech. Their brows furrowed in patterns of perturbation. Without a doubt, Emery had disclosed the details of the dramatic confrontation with the Lennox girl. The tale spread through the castle in a matter of hours, and it was not to be kept from friends of faithfulness.

"Did you bring it?" Ariadne questioned.

"Indeed," I replied, reaching into the satchel around my waist. I retrieved the book of stories that once belonged to my grandmother's imagination. My father's childhood penmanship was scrawled across the corner of the cover page. I flipped to the illustrations of blotted ink and pointed out the pair of identical letters.

"She must be referring to Ms. Ludwig," Emery mused over the initials.

"Well then," said Ariadne, "perhaps this book will provide the perfect source of memories."

Without much time to spare, we caught a ride on the milk wagon that drove away from the kitchen. The old farmer did not seem to mind, and his horses were glad for a few carrots. The roads were rough, as the cart did not travel through the scenic route. Even so, the jaunt was swift.

When we arrived in the village, the farmer tipped his hat and clucked the horses forward. Shades of red appeared on the skyline as the sun began to hide its face. Lydia's cottage was settled on the edge of town, where a band of kittens tumbled through fallen leaves, and vines climbed over the stone walls. The garden was tended with transcendence. There was not a fault to be discovered in the picturesque home.

"Here we are!" Juniper sighed.

We approached the house with confident strides, although others believed the resident to be mad. An old woman opened the door after a single knock, as if she had been waiting for our arrival. Her spectacles were rounder and wider than before, with lenses that magnified her curious eyes.

"Oh, wonderful!" Lydia exclaimed in her delirious voice. "I must admit I've been expecting you—what with all the nonsense of that boarding school! You know, that headmistress really must explore the possibilities of another garden. It would be quite beneficial to your studies with Professor Biddle." The old lady continued to ramble for several minutes.

Ariadne waved her hands in a hushing motion. "Listen," she interrupted. "We are not here to discuss the various breeds of flowers."

"For the second time, I have found the courage to ask for your help," I spoke after nodding in gratitude to my friend. "Although you may not care to admit the truth, you are the only one who can read the memories of my grandmother."

Lydia stood in silence as I handed over the book of fiction. She adjusted her spectacles before focusing on the name of the authoress. Her mouth parted with the intent of speech. Nevertheless, words did not comprehend the emotion that swelled in her chest. A reflective tear escaped her grasp, streaming down her cheek. Unnoticed, it landed on the fabric of her gown. When a minute passed, the woman lifted her gaze and stroked the side of my face.

"Dear Alice," Lydia whispered, "you are so much like Orinthia."

"So I've been told." I twirled a lock of ginger hair. "I'm not sure how much."

"Oh, it's not just your beauty!" Lydia responded. "You are kindred spirits in more ways than one."

Flipping through the illustrated pages, the woman came across the unusual splotches of ink. Her fingers traced the path between each of the letters, smiling as she reached the initials of her name. The grin faded as realization dawned upon her wrinkled face. She placed a feather between the binding before leading us into the drawing room. A calico cat snoozed on the couch, beside a steaming cup of tea. It startled as the woman closed the curtains with haste.

"You must understand that I am risking my life to assist in this endeavor," said Lydia. "While Aisling was formed by the Creator of light, there are both good and bad people in this realm. The Lennox clan would not be pleased to learn about this investigation. Therefore, each of you must keep your mouths shut. Grave danger lurks around the corner, without a doubt."

I glanced at the other girls, searching for a trace of hesitation in their eyes. In seas of green, gray, and blue, there was nothing of the fearful sort, for courage and persistence overwhelmed such emotion.

Lydia removed her spectacles and placed them on the table. The cat resumed his nap as the woman reopened the book of fairy tales. She placed a finger on the beryl ink before looking off into the distance. Her eyes were slightly unfocused, as though she pondered a night of dreams. In truth, she was Gifted with the ability to see beyond, to find and read the memories of others. Although some feared such a power, it was given to a woman with pure intentions, and there are few things more beautiful.

I watched her expression transform with time. A vision leaped behind each moment, as it painted in the brightest colors of truth. A mixture of horror and hope traveled through her stare until there was nothing more than peace. As she returned from a dreamlike state, the woman clasped her hands together in hesitation.

"Oh, the poor child," Lydia whispered. A distant expression was written across her face. It was cold and pale, and full of astonishment. The old woman did not frown with sorrow or speak of abomination. Even so, she appeared to be rather troubled.

"What did you see, Lydia?" I begged.

Her crinkled eyes looked through me, as though she were Gifted with the power to reach through one's soul. She picked up her spectacles and placed them on the bridge of her nose. Like most wise elders, she did not care to pour the details like a cup of tea. Lydia allowed the memories to settle in her mind, as the art of storytelling often requires. She walked across the floor and found a seat on the couch, gesturing for us to do the same. As I sat on my hands, the cat glanced up and released a deep purr. The evening sun was beginning to move onward in order to make way for the starlit night.

"Listen to my words with care," Lydia reminded us, "for not a single element can be omitted from the tale."

We nodded in response.

After taking a delicate sip from her teacup, the elder shared the secrets of history. Words escaped from her mouth with ambivalence. Orinthia's ink-stained memories were captured in the days before the Lost Dreamer vanished on the shores of the Northern Sea. With the assistance of my grandmother, the headmistress had received her position in the Order of Birch, where she worked to improve the opportunities for Gifted children born on lands beyond the realm. It was four years after my birth, when strange creatures began to appear in the forest of oaks. Of course, the curse existed for centuries before this time, but the effects had never before escalated at such a rate.

The Order of Birch was wrapped in consternation, while the Gifted sought to find the source of darkness. Many villagers began to suffer from an unknown fever, which spread like wildfire across the land. It murdered in silence and glazed over the eyes of innocent children.

In an attempt to extinguish the illness, the previous headmaster closed the Academy for a single semester. During this time, the castle was used as an isolation hospital for the unwell. Ariadne and Juniper were too young to hoard sufficient memories of the epidemic, but both recalled teaspoons of herbal remedies and endless hours spent in the solitude of their homes.

The village of Innis was impacted more than the countryside. Some blamed the disease on sailors and pirates docked in the seaport town. Such rumors did not provide a cure. Hundreds died in the plague, while others survived months of trepidation.

The MacMillan clan was unfortunate to lose their daughter, Saoirse, during this time. The poor infant suffered under spells of delirium before she succumbed to the fever. The Gifted people mourned her death for weeks before her brother disappeared on the shore. Although he did not contract the illness, the villagers assumed otherwise. To be sure, feverish delirium was an unproven explanation for his disappearance, and most assumed the child drowned under rough waves.

Dark secrets veiled a terrible truth.

At the time, Sir Lennox was a secluded and sphinxlike man, and his two children were no exception. Cleona was nothing more than a toddler, but the beginning of her life was spent in a household devoid of maternal love. While her father disappeared for weeks at a time, nursemaids raised the dark-haired girl. Her elder brother was already noble and wise beyond his years, as his unusual name suggests. His golden eyes promised of a power in the common rankings, and such was the prize his sister did not receive. The lad did not suffer under the harsh hand and neglect of his father; rather, he accompanied the man on endeavors and learned of the prejudice in his father's heart. It would not be foolish to assume the child learned from the mistakes of his father, while his sister aged with nothing more than a dangerous hunger for acceptance.

In the evenings of summer, between hours spent in the seat of her writing desk, Orinthia tended the rose gardens of Macnas Manor. As a matter of course, Sir Lennox galloped the road on horseback, headed toward the edge of the Night Oak Forest. Orinthia noticed this repeated occurrence, and her suspicions grew with the passing weeks. When the changed seasons brought early nightfall, she followed him on the back of a borrowed mare.

Deep in the Night Oak Forest, an old witch lived amongst the darkness. Her home was built in a fallen tree, far from the haunting creatures of the night. She was educated in the secrets of herbs and potions, which lined the walls of her crowded hut. Though the witch was not covered in boils or cursed with a crooked nose, her powers were misunderstood, and she was doomed to a life of exile.

When Sir Lennox appeared on her doorstep, the elder rushed him forward with a broom. She glanced around for a moment before striking a conversation with the man. As Orinthia listened through an open window, she learned of a sinister promise.

The witch was talented in the art of brewing, and Sir Lennox commissioned her to create a series of strange potions, each to contain the poison of a forbidden herb. In exchange, the man was prepared to hand over his only daughter, for the witch was growing old and needed a successor. Her compassion for the Gifted people was overturned with bitterness, and she did not care about the intentions of the strange man. The witch lived far from the nearest village, and she knew nothing of the unexplainable fever that spread with each potion she brewed for him.

"Perhaps she could have saved them," Lydia spoke with a gentle sigh. "As a matter of routine, the poison was poured into the wells of the village and countryside.

Certain individuals were immune, such as those Gifted with a secondary form. The majority of victims belonged to the 'rare' classification. When your grandmother discovered the truth, she was horrified. That wicked man committed genocide on almost half the population! He possessed an elixir that would prevent his clan from contracting the fever, while the rest of the Gifted people were made to battle the poison. He sought to strip the realm of peculiarities, and leave the survivors to breed a certain kind of power."

"That's impossible!" Ariadne cried. "The Gifts of Aisling are seldom inherited."

"The children of Aisling are created with unique traits and individual beauties," Juniper affirmed. "No person has the power to filter such a truth."

"Ah, you are wise," said Lydia. "The Creator sculpts with the hands of a true artist, as the same soul never forms twice. Sir Lennox was swift to realize this, but it was too late to save the victims of his poison. He succeeded in wiping out a large group of rarities; however, his mission remains incomplete."

For a moment, it seemed as though the tale were nothing more than fiction. After pulling back from the woman's entrancing voice, I stood in a state of silence. A sick feeling settled in the pit of my stomach—a harsh blend of outrage and understanding. Endless questions received answers, as everything began to fall in place.

My grandmother had learned the truth, and she left it for us to share. Danger lingered behind the walls of Castle Moss, preparing to make a lethal advance. To overcome such corruption, we needed to gather support from the people of Aisling, and such a task can only be accomplished through the revelation of verities.

"All Gifts are rare and beautiful, but some people will never understand such a truth." Juniper sighed. "The definition of value has warped with the teachings of Wolfgang Gregory, and failed to restore with the loss of his life in battle."

"Sir Lennox continues to live with an ambition that cannot be justified," Lydia commented. "I've seen his terrible actions with my own eyes. I've known the harm that he is capable of inflicting. This realm survives under the scars of the past, and the future shall bring a great battle."

"Well then," I murmured, "that solves one piece of the puzzle, but there must be a connection between Cleona and the Lost Dreamer. She attempted to keep us from discovering the cavern in the sea. By order of her father, she guards the misdeeds of her clan."

"The Siren Sisters are not to blame for Fionn's stolen childhood," Lydia informed us. "Such was the reality of my disappearance, but nothing happens the same way twice."

"Well," said Ariadne, "elaborate, if you will!"

"Unlike my situation, the Siren Sisters were informed about the strange powers of the fair-haired lad," Lydia explained. "Fionn discovered his talents at an early age. He must've been no more than four years old when his dreams soothed the nightmares of his poor sister. For a while, his Gift was a topic of the local gossip. It was quite an unusual occurrence, as most Gifted children bloom around the age of twelve. The news reached Lennox Manor in a matter of weeks, and the man of the house was not pleased. With the ability to walk in the land of dreams, Fionn threatened to reveal the cause of his sister's death. Sir Lennox sent a message to the dark sirens, to inform them about the strange child. He learned of the lost voices through the tale of my apparent madness. Unlike most of the villagers, Lennox dared to explore the possibilities, and he used the truth to his advantage.

"Perhaps you are surprised to learn that such a monster could fear a toddler with little more than two dozen words of speech," Lydia continued. "You must understand a detail of great significance. While there are rumors of their heritage, the Lennox clan descends from the blood of Wolfgang. His malevolence survives generations, but his prejudice was built upon shoulders of nonsensical fear—and therein lies the weakness, dear girls."

"What do you expect of us?" Ariadne demanded. "These secrets are the products of madness, and we are in over our heads!"

"Oh," said Emery, "I wouldn't be so sure."

"Every villain was once an innocent child," said Lydia. "When the spirit is not tended with care, the glow fades away. Cleona Lennox lives as an example of this statement. Her downfall can be traced to her need for acceptance, and her rise dares to emerge from it as well. As you survive the coming months, watch the girl with care. She is your greatest connection to the plans of her father. In the meantime, the Guardians of Aisling commit their allegiance to the Four Elementals, and few allies are shaped with such value.

"Despite all of the choices in life, so much has already been planned for you. When all seems lost and hopeless, you can find comfort in the knowledge that the greatest power stands beside you," said Lydia. "Keep focused on the valley of stars, dear girls. One day, each of you shall discover the brilliant land that lingers beyond."

CHAPTER TEN

The new sense of knowledge left a weight on my heart. I felt anguish for the Gifted children swept away in a hidden battle. As the breath of autumn transformed into the roar of winter, the festivities of the season contrasted the sorrows. It isn't difficult to fall into a spell of sadness, but such things are often overturned with courage.

There was comfort to be found in the scent of paper, frown of professors, and routine of education. Ronan and Kade participated in nearly all of the same classes, providing me with a sustainable source of amusement. Between lectures and assignments, our sharp quips served as righteous forms of entertainment. Even so, it was impossible to ignore the invisible wall that separated us. My grandmother's memories contained secrets of the past, unknown to other students. The art of timing ruled over the possibilities of revelation.

As I walked across the dining hall, the laughter of students echoed in a haunted tone. Countless children were missing from the crowd, as their lives were interrupted by the poison of antagonism. I sat beside Emery and Kade, before crafting a plate of fresh porridge and lionberries. I held my hands over the bowl until a trail of steam floated overhead.

My sister was engrossed in conversation about the upcoming gala of All Hallows' Eve. The celebration provided her mind with an escape from the burden of memories. It was our seventeenth birthday, of course, and there was much to plan. Emery's face was alight with the mere thought of the elegant ballroom. Her wonder transformed into a childish grin as footsteps approached from behind me.

Without a glance over my shoulder, I recognized the sound of his stride. Ronan walked with a long gait, and never tucked his hands into the pockets of his vest. His voice was swift to announce his arrival, as he mused over the appearance of disgruntled professors.

"Are you looking forward to the celebration, Ronan?" Kade inquired.

"Indeed," Ronan replied, revealing a hint of amusement. "Although I must admit I've been torn between a wide selection of breeches and doublets. Tell me, fair maidens, do you favor silver or golden thread?"

As I batted him on the shoulder, the freckled lad claimed the empty seat beside me. His blue eyes danced in the light of humor. It was the same expression he had worn on the night of the gala at Lennox Manor. While happiness flooded his gaze, a hint of compassion crossed his face, as it was not so difficult to notice the tinge of despair in my voice. He stared at me for a brief moment, as though further analysis might reveal the source of emotion. When I looked back at him, Ronan revealed a simple smile. There was something there, beneath the surface.

The moment was interrupted by a voice at the podium. I turned to greet the dark hair and sapphire gaze of the headmistress. She spoke with a clear accent, announcing the details of the upcoming celebration and harvest weekend. As I watched with care, her unwavering words faded into the background. She stood there, clothed in a fine gown, blind to the historic secrets that dared to spread ruin. With her position of power, she was obligated to hold her attention on the wellbeing of the Gifted people, but she allowed one crisis to slip through her fingers.

Although the emotion was irrational, a flame of anger burned within me. It was not formed against the headmistress; rather, it was dedicated to the trust placed in her character. When I arrived at the Academy for Gifted Youth, it wasn't difficult to honor the woman. She was clever, compassionate, and uncommonly wise. At the same time, she seemed to separate herself from the Elementals, as though she did not wish to associate with those who restored the peace of the Night Oak Forest. I wanted to trust her actions and believe in her reason, like one should believe in a proper leader. A piece of my grandmother's spirit shined from her eyes—a piece that I did not care to forget.

Over the summer, the headmistress spoke of her allegiance, but she stood in silence during the interrogation at Castle Moss. Although she promised to guard us, Professor Hawthorne remained in her study and avoided the chance of confrontation. She spoke in a distant voice, while her gaze focused far above my head. When the speech concluded, she disappeared in the crowd of students. Like others, she hid something from the world.

❧❦❧

Thunder rattled the hardwood floors, waking me from a deep slumber. A flash of light illuminated the night skies before vanishing without a trace. Rubbing the sleep from my eyes, I reached for the vial strung around my neck. A note remained behind the glass, tied in a scroll with faded ribbon. A year had passed since I read the piece of prose for the first time; nevertheless, it seemed like a decade.

As I mused over moments, another rumble of thunder shook the castle walls. A shrill scream followed from the shadows of the night. A touch of fear awoke in my chest. My sister's heavy eyelids did not flinch against the forces of nature. Like Juniper and Ariadne, she snored and dreamed with careless abandon.

I threw back the covers, slipped out of bed, and wandered over to the window. I placed my hands on the iron handle before pushing the panels open wide. Autumn whispered into the chamber, chilled with the breath of the coming rain. I glanced back for a moment. Emery smiled in the comfort of the cold air, while Juniper pulled a quilt around her shoulders.

A russet creature appeared beside the border of the Night Oak Forest. I recognized the sharp muzzle and pointed ears of the red fox. It dashed across the open meadows, heading straight for the castle entrance. A lantern followed close behind, along with the arrows of a skilled archer. The fox released a sharp howl, which pierced through the fog of midnight.

Killian.

I pressed a hand my lips, which parted in a gasp of silence. All traces of sleep vanished from my eyes, as consciousness returned with sudden force. Without a second thought, I grabbed the cloak from my wardrobe and rushed through the chamber doors. A flickering lamp illuminated the corners of Lancaster Hall. Shadows collected around the furniture and countless stacks of books. The lull of slumber seemed to drift under each of the chamber doors, spreading out over the common room. A single door stood ajar, revealing the faint light of a wax candle.

As I stepped into the corridor, it was impossible to muffle the echo of footsteps on the marble floors. My heart pounded against my chest, begging to leap forward. My nightgown was sure to be mistaken for that of a ghost in the passage, as the hem floated around my bare ankles.

I swept down the grand stairwell and into the entrance hall. Dust drifted through the air, imitating the wild dance of faeries, while the silver moonlight shone upon my face. My attention turned toward the small prints of mud that trailed away from the doors.

"Alice," a curious voice spoke from the corner. "I've been waiting for you."

Killian stepped into the light. There was not a trace of fear in his expression, but there was courage to be found in his gaze. His muzzle was scratched and trickled with blood; however, his pelt was untouched by arrows.

"What are you doing here?" I demanded. "I heard your scream and noticed your pursuer through the chamber windows."

"Oh, never mind that!" the fox dismissed.

"But I shall," I responded. "You could've been shot with an arrow! Where are the other Guardians, and what trouble have you caused?"

The fox remained silent for a moment before trotting toward the stairwell. His ears pricked forward in attention. "Someone's coming," he snapped.

I glanced around in panic, in search of a suitable place to hide. A broom closet caught my attention before the sound of footsteps echoed above our heads. The fox followed me in haste, knocking down empty buckets in the process. His golden eyes peered through the darkness.

A shadow fell over the gap in the door as a figure moved across the entrance hall. Leather boots and raven-black hair reflected the light of the crescent moon. I recognized the bold brows and dauntless stride of the Lennox girl. She turned down the corridor with a care-lessness that vexed me.

"Where is she going?" Killian asked.

"Perhaps we will find out," I whispered before stepping out of the closet. "In the meantime, you will be kind enough to explain that frantic run through the forest."

The ginger fox rolled his eyes as he followed me through the ancient halls. Cleo's shoes echoed in the distance as we followed several steps out of sight. A few minutes passed before we reached the quadrangle, where the castle walls surrounded a small courtyard. Constellations flickered above the remaining flowers, which cowered against the breath of midnight.

"I didn't have a look at the archer—at least not enough to recognize him," said Killian. "A creature of less cleverness might assume it was a simple hunter, unaware of the Gifted nature of his target. Nevertheless, such lack of intelligence has never burdened me."

"You are not so talented in the art of hiding suspicion." I glanced around in a careful manner.

"Certainly not," Killian replied with a curled grin. After a long pause, the fox spoke once more. "Ms. Ludwig was wise enough to share her concerns about your grandmother's ink-stained memories."

"Oh, really?" I turned on my heels to face him. Despite my efforts, the mere thought leaked through reflective tears. "Then you must have been insensitive enough to bother the poor woman."

"Dear Alice," the Guardian spoke, allowing his voice to drop in a low tone. "Listen to me, please. Although the knowledge of the crime was isolated until now, such a fact does not discount the value of human life. The Gifted people deserve to know the truth, and the Lennox clan must suffer the consequences of their actions. For several months, the Guardians of Aisling have speculated about the infiltration of the Order of Birch. It will not be denied. Your grandmother's memories have brought forth a forgotten battle, one that cannot be ignored."

The conversation hushed as we caught sight of a figure that moved through the darkness. Cleona turned around the corner and halted in front of a tapestry. A dark cloak covered her head, nearly hiding a passive expression. Pulling back the woven material, she revealed the bare wall. She placed a hand against one of the cobblestones, pushing it inward with the slightest touch. Something shifted in the castle walls, before a hidden passage appeared in its place. The girl glanced over her shoulder, before disappearing into the shadows.

"Where is she going?" I whispered.

"Cleona has discovered the maze of passageways that hide in this castle. Based on the confidence and direction of her stride, it would not be foolish to assume she is bound for the forest. This section travels under-ground," said Killian. "Most students learn about the secret halls that line the main corridors, but few have entered and used it to their advantage. The passages are not simple to navigate, and only the headmistress possesses a proper map."

"Are you sure?"

"Of course." Killian nodded with assurance. "Unless it has been replicated or stolen from her desk."

"Doubtful," I responded. "It seems like that woman never leaves her chambers. There was a time when she roamed the libraries and stepped into classrooms. She used to smile and laugh with the students. There was a time when I looked up to her, as one might look up to an elder sister. Such days have passed, and my respect for her character has dwindled like a flame."

"Oh, Alice," Killian spoke, turning his head to look at me. "You have lost faith in the faithful. Have you forgotten the promise that lingers between Zara and Orinthia? Do you remember the sacrifices the headmistress made for you? Like the Guardians of Aisling, she seeks your protection."

"Well then," I replied, "Hawthorne spoke of her promise to my grandmother, but she doesn't seem too concerned about keeping it. In the greatest times of trial, the headmistress does not care to speak more than a few words to me. Her loyalties are uncertain."

"Oh, no," Killian murmured. His eyes widened with sudden realization. "She didn't tell you."

"Tell me what?"

"As you know well, Professor Hawthorne holds an influential position in the Order of Birch. Since its recent infiltration, she has been accused of working against foundational principles of the Academy for Gifted Youth," Killian explained. "Such accusations are absurd, of course, but few people dare to question the words of Sir Bastian Amulet. As a result, the headmistress must be careful with her actions."

"That's madness!" I exclaimed.

"She has been accused of placing the Elementals above her loyalties to the realm," Killian insisted.

"What does it matter, when the Elementals have performed nothing but acts of courage, all in order to save this land from destruction?" I responded. "Like the other girls, I did not expect to be the heroine of this tale. It was the right of my birth, the answer to an ancient prophecy."

"Whether it pleases you or not, each of you are rare, even in the land of the Gifted," Killian snapped. "Such titles are not always received with open arms. While the elements of nature restored the light of the forest, the plot of darkness was diminished, not destroyed. Maintain your guard, freckled one. The future looms ahead, veiled in uncertainty, and you must meet it with courage."

CHAPTER ELEVEN

The future did arrive, as it always does; however, it did not greet me with a courteous bow. It lingered in the entrance of my life, waiting for the perfect moment to step into the land of consciousness, when I might begin to acknowledge the changes that stemmed from ages past. Between classes, I mused over the upcoming gala and found myself ashamed, for it was trivial in comparison to the newfound secrets.

Students traveled home for the weekend, as families prepared for the coming month of winter. Some left with eagerness, while others departed in hesitation. In less than a week, the castle was bound to be decorated for the final festivities of autumn.

The roads were lined with horses, which processed in a slow fashion. Children danced and laughed as if nothing had changed. Warm smiles and bright eyes greeted the students with open arms, as families gathered into the coaches.

I stood on the edge of the castle steps, lost in a haze of scattered thoughts. Ariadne and Emery spoke in hushed tones, while Juniper sat in the emerald grass. In spite of everything, there was little to discuss. Kade and Ronan assisted their father with the luggage, while a pair of carriage horses sighed with disinterest.

"Alice," Juniper spoke, "I don't see your parents in the distance. Are you traveling with another student?"

"Indeed," I replied. "The O'Reilly clan has been kind enough to offer us a place in their carriage."

"Oh, lovely!" the wild-haired girl responded, tossing a swift glance at Ronan. Her expression brimmed with the sort of amusement that raises a single brow.

"There are some things I will never understand about him." I kneeled down beside my friend. "He does everything right, but he doesn't have any previous experience when it comes to relationships. As for my part, I know nothing more than theories of his intentions. His friendship has settled in the corners of my heart."

"Perhaps you are not so difficult to read." Juniper smiled. "Do not fear your emotions, Alice, for such things cannot be kept inside. Feelings are destined for the freedom of flight, in the same way the truth is bound to be revealed."

"There is a proper time and place for such freedom," I responded. "And I have yet to find it."

"Time is wasted in the art of waiting," Juniper said. She turned to look at me with a thoughtful expression.

"Sometimes, the perfect moment stands before you, and it requires nothing more than an ounce of faith."

"Well then," I whispered, "I am not the only person to seek sincerity."

"Certainly not," Juniper affirmed, allowing her emerald gaze to drift toward the carriage horses. "But I believe it has arrived without your recognition."

I glanced over my shoulder with slight hesitation. A strange realization dawned upon me. It was quite unexplainable, though it spoke in a lucid tone. As Ronan lifted the final trunk into the coach, his blue gaze caught on mine. He held it there until a freckled smile spread across his face. His attention swiftly redirected as his father clapped him on the back.

A quilted landscape blurred into the background of the Academy for Gifted Youth. Sweeping gowns and bursts of laughter embodied the essence of the changing seasons. Juniper and Ariadne departed the castle on horseback, each one cutting through opposite paths in the forest.

"All aboard!" Mr. O'Reilly shouted over the melody of conversation. He leaped for the reins with unexpected spirit.

I stepped into the carriage and claimed the seat beside my sister. Her blue eyes focused on the horses that trailed down the dirt road. There was much to think about, and few words to speak. Ronan was squashed against the wings of his sister, although he did not seem to mind. Kade was cloaked in feathers of elegance, which gleamed in the vivid light of the evening.

When the carriage arrived at Macnas Manor, my spirit released a sigh of ease. The stone walls and wild gardens seemed to whisper words of welcome. A pair of horses grazed in the pastures that swept over the hillside. Although it was not the white farmhouse that claimed so many years of childhood, the old manor represented home. A single summer had acquainted me with its hidden libraries, chambers, and kindred portraits. The house was fit for endless hours of exploration.

"Here we are," said Emery.

We thanked the O'Reilly clan and approached the entrance of the stone house. The blue door was slightly chipped, and garden soil littered the edge of the steps. These faults were more than beautiful to me. Emery reached out to rap her knuckles on the wood, but the door swung open before she had the chance.

"Oh, my sweet girls!" our mother exclaimed, before flinging her arms around us. "I have missed you more than words can describe."

After several moments of laughter and tears, she gathered us into the house and waved to the coachman with a gesture of gratitude. As I stepped through the door, the scent of warm bread and firewood swept over me. A shadow moved down the length of the corridor, before stepping into the light.

My father looked upon his daughters with unmasked delight. "And I don't suppose you have missed your old man." His blond hair was beginning to turn white, along with his ungroomed beard. A glint of humor hid behind his cerulean eyes, the same eyes that belonged to my sister.

"More than you can imagine," I replied.

CHAPTER TWELVE

Morning gleamed beyond the chamber windows, passing through translucent curtains. I squinted against the light, attempting to sleep for just a few more minutes. This wish was swiftly denied as Emery tossed an old slipper over my head. I removed the quilt that covered my eyes and turned to glare at her in annoyance.

"Time to rise and shine!" She tumbled out of bed and danced across the hardwood floor. "After breakfast, we must unload the gowns from the attic. Tomorrow brings our seventeenth birthday and the celebration of All Hallows' Eve. I haven't found a chance to glance at those dresses in the old wardrobe."

"I'm sure you will find one in a suitable shade of blue." A trickle of laughter escaped from me, even while thoughts drifted elsewhere.

"Very well," Emery replied. "Then we must find something for *you* to wear! Juniper is quite talented in the art of plaiting, and I'm sure she will be able to weave a bit of ribbon through your mane. There was a rouge gown in our grandmother's collection, and I have no doubt it will complement the hues of your ginger hair!"

"Oh, hush!" I groaned. "For the past week, have you thought about anything more than this extravagant ball? *Honestly,* Emery! A terrible darkness creeps through this realm, unseen in the shadows of the past. You have always been the sincere sister, so concerned about others. Hundreds of children have perished at the hands of the Lennox clan. Are you not haunted by the memories our grandmother left behind?"

Emery stared back at me with an unreadable expression. Her round eyes held a look of dismay, while a touch of heartbreak seeped through her parted lips. She stood there, in her nightgown, rubbing traces of sleep away from her lashes. A single tear streamed down her cheek before she caught it with the hope of it being unseen.

We seldom fought, even throughout our synchronized childhood. Despite our differences, our sisterhood was built upon the grounds of awareness. Unlike so many others, our relationship was valued more than trivial matters. The fear of losing each other always outweighed fleeting anger.

"Alice," Emery spoke, allowing her voice to crack with sorrow. "If you think otherwise, you are nothing more than a fool. I've scarcely been able to sleep through the night, and one cannot blame this on ominous dreams.

The peace of Aisling proves to be a facade, which covers the unknown truth. I imagine the faces of those children. The mere image weighs my spirit down like an anchor in the sea. So, I pray you will forgive my frivolous distractions."

Emery rushed out of the bedroom and slammed the door shut. I listened to the sound of her bare feet running down the corridor. A prick of guilt touched my heart, which begged me to follow the girl. Nevertheless, it was not a wise notion, for we needed time to settle in our own thoughts.

The memories tormented our gentle minds, driving us to find solace in simple diversions. No person deserves to suffer under such knowledge, but things never change without confrontation.

In truth, it was real—the sorrow, the pain, and the remorse felt for the loss of the Gifted. The simple rarity of their existence was enough to prompt wonder, followed by the darkness of misconception.

I slipped out of bed and changed into a proper riding gown. A chestnut mare waited beside the walled pastures, prepared for a gallop through the fields. As I approached with tack in hand, she pawed the ground with anticipation.

I attempted to shut out the sting of the argument, the guilt that settled in my chest. *Emery should be standing beside me; she should be challenging me to a race across the moorlands.* Instead, she wept behind the windows of her chamber and locked the door before our mother had the chance to enter. Her room was bound to frost over, as she did not care for an intrusion.

I pulled the last buckle taut and swung over the back of the horse. Felicity's ears flicked back after a few moments, as she waited for the next signal. I pressed her forward with persistence. Dirt crunched beneath her hooves, which created a trail of prints in the earth.

I didn't care to think much about the celebration of the season, even while it brought much excitement to the hearts of others. Of course, the gala was destined to be a grand affair. As I rode through the fields, the strides became a dance, and the fields transformed into a ballroom. I shut my eyes against the sun and imagined the light of chandeliers.

The next day promised to bring my seventeenth birthday, along with that of three friends. Was it a turn of fate that brought the Elementals into this world at the same hour? Perhaps... but such wonders are rarely of mere coincidence.

I felt like a little girl hidden behind the character of a woman—tired, restless, and brimming with dreams. I wanted to scream into the wilderness with careless abandon, unconcerned about the future. I wanted to stand in the open fields with my arms stretched out against the wind. It was a fantastic notion of freedom; however, it was not so realistic.

Secrets wandered through my mind, each one waiting for the proper moment to escape. My fingers burned against leather reins. The truth begged to be shared with the headmistress, for she was destined to call out the maleficence of Lennox. The Order of Birch was sure to believe in the tale, so long as it was spoken from the mouth of Professor Hawthorne. For reasons unknown, their trust wavered over the four girls of elemental powers.

All at once, I returned from a dreamlike daze. Felicity seemed unconcerned, shaking her mane against the breeze. I spurred her forward beside the birch forest, where spotted bark peered through a sea of golden leaves.

"Alice Hanley?"

Glancing over my shoulder, I noticed a horseman trotting through the woods. His head was covered with a tweed cap, while his hands were gloved in leather. He sat astride a dappled mare, who murmured as the pair approached. His features were impossible to mistake, from the simple placement of his shoulders, to the smile that split his freckled face.

"Good morning, Ronan!" I greeted him with surprise.

"And same to you, Niamh."

"I didn't expect to find you here," Ronan said. "Our Creator works in mysterious ways."

"Certainly," I responded. "What brings you to this side of the forest?"

"Believe it or not," Ronan replied, "I am on route to the house of the tailor. I was prepared to inquire at the doors of Macnas Manor, as it stands on the backroad to the village."

"Oh, whatever for?"

"To speak with you," Ronan spoke in a careful tone, unaware of the color that tinted his cheeks. "And request your company at the ball."

I stared at him for a moment, which stretched out in an uncomfortable manner. His gaze did not divert from mine. My lips parted with the intention of speech, but the proper response did not arrive with ease.

I did not expect to receive an invitation, as few students accompanied each other to the gala. It was often a matter of breaking the barrier that separates each side of the ballroom. Within the first hour, several couples were bound to glide across the floor, like swans on the surface of Loch Dairbhreach. Before the final set, all sensible ladies were bound to lounge against the walls.

"Well then," Niamh interrupted the silence. "Respond to the lad, dear girl! I've little patience for this sort of tension."

"This invitation is untimely, to be sure," Ronan added with sudden hesitation. "Regardless of your answer, please know that it will be acknowledged with my respe—"

"Yes," I interrupted.

"What?"

"I'm pleased to accept your invitation."

My friend looked up with an unexpected expression. A brilliant smile overwhelmed his face. Happiness poured over him—like sunlight over dawn—until it reached my spirit.

My mind raced through an eternal fog, as though the moment were nothing more than a work of the imagination. My hands wished to reach for the collar of his jacket, to feel the rough material under my skin. Such an action might prove the reality of the situation, or pull me away from a peculiar dream. To counter this idea, my fingers combed through the mare's mane.

"In that case," said Ronan, "I shall meet you on the castle steps."

CHAPTER THIRTEEN

My hands ran over the golden gown that rested across the bed. It was crafted from the finest silk, a rare sort to find in the marketplace of the modern age. The design was unusual yet elegant, and it suited my character in more ways than one. Translucent ribbon streamed down the sleeves, which puffed around both elbows. It was the work of my great-grandmother, the woman responsible for the tapestries and photographs that lined the corridors. She was known for the expanse of her creative mind.

A thin layer of clouds settled over the horizon. For the first time in weeks, my mind was at peace. It was the first hours of my seventeenth birthday, the silver dawn of All Hallows' Eve.

The scent of my mother's perfume lingered in the air, surrounded with a bundle of fresh waterlilies. That woman sensed the tension between her twin daughters and sought to mend a precious bond. With her sense of style, she pulled apart the attic wardrobes. A pair of fine gowns were made to be shared, especially in preparation for a fine occasion.

While Emery avoided all conversation at dinner, she did not dwell in silence at the breakfast table. Anticipation dripped like honey from her lips, gathered in soft and careful words. She admired the curls of my hair and begged for assistance in the task of braiding. It was not long before the tension dissolved into unspoken forgiveness.

My mind continued to reel from the encounter beside the forest. Of course, Ronan was a loyal friend, and there was no reason to feel strange about his invitation. He was kind-hearted, and there was no evidence to suggest that his words contained deeper emotion. Would it not be foolish to assume otherwise?

I was not sure.

And so, the world was left to wonder.

As I stood before the golden gown, a thin figure appeared in the doorway of the chamber. Emery looked around with care. Her gaze was laced with fascination.

"Please," I spoke, "come in."

As Emery stepped into the light, a waterfall of tulle appeared around her waist. Yellow hair flowed in waves over her shoulders. She was dressed in a gown of sapphire, which complemented the cold tones of her eyes.

"Oh, Emery!" I gasped. "You are far too enchanting, even for one of this realm."

A gentle smile formed across her lips, while memories of our shared childhood danced through my mind. In the earliest years of life, we read tales of magic and darkness, but we never imagined the truth of the stories. We dressed in the costumes of faeries and trolls, though it was nothing more than an act of make-believe. Our Gifts transformed the matter of our lives. The tale of magic was no longer a work of fiction, for most everything was real.

"Have you spoken to the O'Reilly twins?" Emery asked. "Kade inquired about assistance with Juniper's mane. I haven't found a chance to respond to her letter. With those Stone curls, I am sure it will take forever to work through the task."

"Yes," I responded. "Ronan crossed the riding path beside the White Birch Forest."

"Did you speak to him?"

"Of course."

"Well then?" Emery insisted. Her pale brows furrowed with sudden interest. "What did you speak about?"

"Nothing of your concern," I replied in a smooth tone. But she did not take these words for an answer. Silence settled over the chamber, until the fair-haired girl stood before me. She placed her hands on her waist, in order to mark her place on the floor. The typical traits of grace and introversion seemed to vanish from her character. She stared at me with round eyes, which dared to reach for the conversation that pressed on my mind.

"Oh, you must tell me!" Emery cried. "Otherwise, it will weigh down on my spirit, and trust will evaporate from this sisterhood."

"Don't be ridiculous." I sighed.

"I never keep secrets from you!" she persisted.

"*Fine.*"

A sudden look of contentment washed over her face. She hurried across the wood floors and sat beside the bed.

"If you must know," I spoke in a low tone, "Ronan has requested my company at the ball."

"Oh, Alice!" Emery exclaimed, overcome with pure rapture. She rested her chin over her knuckles. "How lovely! You must tell me the details. However did he ask you?"

"Just as I told you," I replied, waving a hand in a manner of dismissal. "Don't fuss over it. Ronan means nothing more than kindness—and friendship. He cares to ensure a reliable dance partner. After all, half of the first-year girls are mad for him. The poor lad is not so gifted in the art of flirtation."

"Now you're being ridiculous, Alice!" Emery stifled a burst of laughter. "Can you not see through him?"

"What do you mean?" I demanded, aware of the blood that rushed to my cheeks.

In truth, the answer was obvious.

❧❧

As I wandered down the old staircase, the sun made way for the moon, casting brilliance over the evening skies. My sister waited in the entrance of the house,

114

accompanied by our parents. Father was dressed in a proper tailcoat, as he prepared to drive a pair of carriage horses toward the castle. When the wood groaned under my footsteps, each of them turned to face me. Sunlight beamed over the gown, reflected on the smiles of three beloved souls.

"Sweet Alice!" Mother sighed. "You are positively radiant."

I smiled in return.

"Happy birthday, my dear girls," Father spoke with a smile. He looked upon his daughters with affection, as well as a trace of wistfulness. Perhaps it was the moment that comes to pass between every parent and child, when the former realizes how much the latter has grown. As Emery stood beside me, this realization seemed to dawn upon our father's countenance. It was not an expression of sorrow; rather, his face seemed to glow with pride. We stood in fine gowns and pearls, though such attire was nothing but material, and such things do not bring much use to the human soul. My father's admiration was found in the courage and compassion of his children.

As the coach carried us toward the castle, Emery rested with both hands upon her chin. I gazed into the forest beyond the glass, hoping to catch a glimpse of the Guardians that followed like shadows. There was comfort in the presence of the archers, for the warriors expressed the truth of their allegiance. Each of the Elementals learned to trust them as one might trust their own clan.

A sudden flash of red caught my attention. Killian was never far from the walls of Macnas Manor. He was obligated to guard the Hanley sisters from danger. I was fond of the notion that his actions resulted from more than onus. There was an element of warmth in his heart, even while he attempted to keep it hidden. In the presence of the fox, there was nothing to fear. His loyalty was evident, and his courage unquestionable. Killian was not a simple Guardian, but he proved to be a fine counselor and steadfast companion.

"A knot has formed in my stomach," Emery murmured, drawing her attention away from the glass. She held her hands together with care. Her cheeks were flushed peony-pink. "It's a terrible feeling that refuses to fade."

"Oh, Emery." I shifted closer to her side of the leather seat. "What bothers you?"

"I cannot tell, for words are not enough to explain," she responded with a light sigh. "I've thought about writing a poem, but such emotions call for the keys of a piano."

"Whatever do you mean?" I asked with a slight frown.

"Are you so oblivious to the admirations of a kindred spirit?" Emery questioned. "You are so fortunate to have an admirer of the overt nature, but you refuse to acknowledge him. You never dare to glance over the walls of your heart, and few people can imagine the pain that comes with such reservations. The poor lad is fond of you, Alice! From the flush of your cheeks, it would not be foolish to assume that you share the same feelings.

While you stand in an indecisive state, the brightest dreams travel through my mind. I've lived in Ronan's shoes, and the soles are far from comfortable."

"Fionn," I whispered, allowing his name to slip through lips with realization. "You're fond of him."

"Yes," Emery laughed. "And perhaps I have always been."

"You claim I am blind to the admirations of another," I replied after a long moment, "but you float in the same boat. Without oars or sails, it refuses to move forward until the wind urges the tide onward."

As evening fell into the hands of the night, stone castles appeared in the distance. Candlelight flickered in the narrow windows, casting streams through the darkness. A trail of coaches and mounted riders lined the road, while each of the horses moved forward with haste. Apprehension ran over my arms. It was a sudden and unexpected reaction, which remained until the carriage halted. My father swung open the door as laughter and conversation flooded through the entrance.

I stepped out with the help of his hand, careful not to trip over the hem of my gown. Emery followed close behind. The castle steps were crowded with unrecognizable silhouettes. It was difficult to watch the carriage leave, as unknown encounters loomed before us. Golden light poured through the entrance, illuminating the gown of a certain dark-haired girl. Although her face was unseen, electric sparks glimmered through the shadows. With a sweep of her dress, she turned toward the entrance hall.

"She's here," I groaned.

"Of course." Emery sighed. "Don't let her mere presence bother you. For this night, focus on something other than those terrible memories. When dawn arrives, you shall return to such mysteries."

We entered the castle behind a trail of Gifted students and dancers. The entrance hall was decked with banners and garlands, which displayed the familiar crest of the Academy for Gifted Youth. A fierce lion and unicorn reared in symbolic battle. Streamers flowed through the air as children sprinted across the floors. The rhythm of pipes and drums reverberated through the crowded corridors. Amidst the beautiful chaos, a violin sang the sharp tune of a reel.

I glanced around for a long moment, overwhelmed by the wealth of festivities. Voices bounced against the walls, reaching my ears with slight amusement.

As I approached the grand hall, the source of music was discovered. A sea of colorful gowns swayed in waves across the dancefloor. My sister drifted into the heart of the celebration, and I followed with the persistence of a shadow.

As we moved across the floor, conversations hushed and students turned to glance in our direction. Even so, this attention did not remain. Ariadne and Juniper emerged from the assemblage, crowned in flowers and tangled vines. The latter danced across the hall with delight, while the former trailed behind with sensible composure.

"Oh, there you are!" said Juniper. "We've been waiting for your arrival. The opening pavane lacked a distinct essence without you."

Emery rolled her eyes with laughter, for the traditional steps did not suit her style. She preferred to twirl with careless abandon, unconcerned with the judgements of others. "Perhaps you refer to my unfiltered lack of grace," she suggested.

"Happy birthday to both of you!" I smiled, whilst careful to move the conversation forward.

"And to you, as well!" Ariadne replied.

"Seventeen is a strange age," Juniper remarked. "It leaves one balanced on the border of adulthood, with their back turned to years of innocent memories."

"I turned away from those years long ago," Ariadne spoke, before shifting her glance toward Lennox.

Cleona was surrounded by a throng of two-faced girls, each one beguiled by the mere promise of shadows. I did not recognize their faces, and it wasn't difficult to propose the trick of an illusion. Four students knew the truth of her father's crimes. The others were wise enough to distrust her character. Cleo's stare burned against me. I turned to meet it without fear. Her arrogance ignited flames that boiled the blood in my veins.

Did she know the truth?

Cleo flinched before her gaze wavered toward the other side of the ballroom. As I turned to greet a familiar face, the feeling of ire faded into oblivion. Juniper and Ariadne dragged my sister across the room, determined to leave the interaction to me. Emery hummed a light tune, sneaking a grin as she passed.

"Ah, if it isn't *an cailín rua*," Ronan addressed me. He was dressed in a simple yet elegant waistcoat, covered by a gold-threaded doublet. A wreath of white blossoms held in his hands.

"Very well then," I replied with slight amusement. "It seems your invitation was not an attempt to paint me as a foolish girl."

"It was most sincere," Ronan affirmed with a dimpled smile. His voice held a trace of defense, for the accusation was rather harsh. "And I hope the celebration will exceed your expectations, if you should have more than one." Without hesitation, he placed the crown of wildflowers on my head of ginger curls. His eyes focused on the petals before shifting back to me. "I suppose this would be the proper time to wish you a happy birthday."

That moment stretched out in a graceful manner, as though all hours of the day sighed in inferiority. Seven o'clock rang with an echo, which shattered the stillness of time.

"Thank you, Ronan."

"For what?"

"For the invitation… for the crown… for the kindness and respect. Ever since that morning at Miller's Bridge, you've always been there for me." I allowed the words to escape without the filter of concern. "You never pressure others, and accept—never expect—so much of me."

Ronan stood there for a long moment, musing over the collection of words. His eyes beamed with something pure, and I found solace in the simple reaction. He didn't know about the hidden memories and secrets of the past. The truth was bound to be revealed with time. When there was darkness to meet, it would be greeted with swords unsheathed. Nevertheless, the freedom of celebration belonged to this night, and it was not a crime for one to indulge in the fleeting hours.

"Shall we?"

Ronan held out his right hand in a courteous gesture. He adjusted his collar as other students turned to stare. There was not a trace of doubt in his gaze. I placed my left hand over his palm, taking notice of his quizzical brow. As we stepped into the ballroom, a ripple of whispers spread out before us.

Cleona stood at the center, engulfed in the conversation of her foolish companions. She was unable to kindle a fire in words of little worth.

"Your hair is sparking again," Ronan remarked, dusting an ember off his shoulder.

"I can't help it," I said. "The entire room watches me, and it makes my skin crawl."

"Well then, you mustn't be ashamed," Ronan spoke in a confident tone, allowing his voice to drift across the room. "For flaws are beautiful differences that have been wrongly considered."

"Not long ago, these flames were the bane of my existence." I turned to face him between the rows of dancers. "As days pass, I continue to release that resentment. I am grateful for the fire that runs through these veins."

My attention drifted several places down the line, where Juniper and Violet tossed grins toward me. Their brows raised in childish amusement, which did nothing to settle my nerves.

Nicholas Stone was seated on a platform on the far side of the hall. I watched as he raised the fiddle to his chin before striking the beginning of a glorious tune. After a few moments, one of the musicians tapped her foot on the ground, and others began to join in the swift reel. A swirling haze of color transformed our surroundings, as the dance moved across the floor. With each sharp note, the crowd cheered until the entire ballroom erupted in an ancient ballad.

Well, once there was a fair young lad.
He roamed down to the sea,
And came across a green mermaid,
Who brought him down for tea.

She was a weary, dark mermaid.
Strange creature, she was swift.
She drank it from a silver glass,
And gave our lad a gift.

The brightest pair of eyes, you see,
Bright scales and emerald fins.
Poor prince became a little fish,
Destined to swim the sea of kings.

The dance faded with the final note. Although the chorus was both poetic and jubilant, it haunted the human spirit. Lyrics bellowed from the lungs of men and women, traveling through the wake of a forgotten summer. My thoughts shifted back to the memories of a dark cavern and dappled sea. Several months had passed since that fateful dawn. It never failed to return in nightmares.

Fionn stood on the other side of the ballroom, along with Emery and Ariadne. His smile teemed with laughter; his hair was trimmed to a proper length. A silent strength replaced the illness that once crept through his body and mind. The lad was tired of the sympathies that followed him like shadows. He spoke of his desire to move forward, to replace his stolen childhood with a brilliant future. Nevertheless, it was difficult to forget the past, for countless secrets dwelled within it.

"Alice?" Ronan's voice shattered my thoughts. "Are you feeling well?"

"Oh, yes," I responded after a short pause.

"Shall we retire?" he asked. "Your face looks rather pale."

I glanced around and noticed the change in our surroundings. A *céilí* dance was beginning to form in the center of ballroom. I stood as an obstacle, staring off in a dreamlike fashion. A fiddle hummed as the tune transformed into a slow jig. I nodded in response and swayed toward the edge of the hall. Ronan followed with careful strides. Despite the vibrancies of the crowd, he never seemed to take his eyes away from me.

A bit of laughter escaped as my attention trailed over the hall. "Grayson's jacket matches the linen," I observed before gesturing to the student clad in red.

"An unusual choice of attire," Ronan affirmed. "Although I must admit it suits his character."

I shrugged as a pocket of silence settled between the music and conversation. It lingered between us, while other students drowned in the entertainment of the night.

Something was wrong. Despite the grand occasion and reason to celebrate, a dire essence lingered under the surface.

Ariadne sauntered through the crowd, accompanied by a stranger of familiar features. His golden-brown hair reflected the warmth of candlelight. His brown eyes were gentle yet full of persistence. From the look of her expression, Ariadne was slightly annoyed and partially amused. She glanced back at the fellow with a swift flick of her hair before continuing an inaudible conversation. Her heart was beginning to shed the armor that it had carried for so long.

Cleo stood in the center of the hall. She watched me with a pensive gaze. Her presence ignited a series of terrible visions—innocent children stolen from this realm. It sparked a ruthless flame. I wished to forget about the memories and dark secrets of our ancestors, even for a single night. Amidst the emotion, children dashed across the ballroom, twirling ribbons over their heads. Their laughter beheld the heart of the celebration.

"Enough with this silence!" I proclaimed, breaking away from a turbulent train of thought. "This is a night of celebration, and it deserves to be treated as such."

Ronan turned to glance at me with a curious expression. His blue eyes laced with the sort of emotion that crinkles around the edges of a smile. Without a word, the lad held out his hand and waited for me to return the gesture. A bit of laughter escaped as we dashed across the room.

I followed him into the entrance hall. Midnight called in a chilled whisper, which promised of freedom and translucence. I did not have the power to resist such temptation. As we reached the doorsteps of the castle, an autumn breeze kissed our cheeks with hesitation. I stepped into the open air, careful to unclasp our hands with grace.

Ronan did not speak a word as he remained under the arched entrance. Moonlight covered his face in shadows, illuminating the smooth curve of his chin. All colors faded under the silver bath of stars. He stood there, unwilling to interrupt the wonders of nature.

"Have you ever screamed into the silence of the night?" I inquired, ever so conscious of the warmth in his gaze.

"Once or twice," Ronan replied in a solemn tone.

"It clears the mind in times of hardship," I continued in a formal manner. "For the spirit requires release from the weights of life."

"To be sure." Ronan descended the castle steps. "In my experience, such action expresses the vehemence of words left unspoken."

I looked at him for a long moment, unsure of the intention behind his statement. Nevertheless, it was not so difficult to guess. He did not remove his gaze from mine. A space between our hearts seemed to close without consciousness. I felt the change settle in my soul—and it terrified me.

Ronan rushed forward into the night and released a fearsome howl. I followed his example and screamed into the eternal land of stars. Our voices were not heard over the hum of music, which floated through the castle windows. All melancholic feelings escaped through the prolonged screech, which faded into the enchanted wilderness.

"In this world of magic and fascination, darkness hides in strange places," I murmured. "It never fails to trouble me."

"All things true are crafted by the hands of the Creator," said Ronan. "All things beautiful and imperfect. The twilight shall not remain for long, for it has a minor role in His plan."

"Perhaps," I whispered. "And there is solace to be found in the truth of our faith."

CHAPTER FOURTEEN

That night continued long after the carriage returned to Macnas Manor. I abandoned a heap of fine fabric and redressed in a tattered nightgown. My sister crawled under the quilts, alight with the excitement of the evening. She spoke with hints of an innocent love, which seemed to form before my eyes. As I told her about the stars that danced in favor, a smile spread across her porcelain face. She teased the notion of friendship with Ronan. My thoughts shifted back to the shadows that laced across his freckled face. A bit of laughter filtered through my voice, which shared the tale of the glorious night.

"Happy birthday, my dear sister," Emery said. "For seventeen years, it has been a wonder to live beside you.

I pray this realm knows the value of your heart… for you deserve a true and faithful love."

An orange glow settled under the surface of my palms, spreading a faint light across the chamber. Emery watched for a moment before moving her left hand into a shadow against the covers. Her lips spread into a careful smile, as her fingertips formed the comical imitation of a wild hare. It was a moment of innocence, which dared to bring back the days of our childhood.

"It's a strange feeling," I murmured, "to recognize an unknown fate."

"It's rather peaceful, I think," said Emery, "to know the fate of the realm does not rest in your hands."

A long while passed before I found the courage to speak again. "Oh, Emery," I whispered. "We really must tell the headmistress; she deserves to know the truth."

She turned to look at me with hesitation. All traces of light vanished from her eyes, along with the glow beneath my palms. "You're right," she huffed. "I've been thinking about it for ages. I didn't care to ruin this night of celebration."

"We cannot fight this battle alone," I murmured. "Professor Hawthorne has lost much of my trust. There are few people left to turn toward for guidance. She knows more about the history of this realm than I have learned over these years."

"You must learn to trust in her promise to our grandmother," said Emery. "I have no doubt she will be faithful to her word."

"Very well then." I sighed. "Perhaps you can explain the reason she left the Elementals in months of silent unrest. We are not alone in this struggle; the Guardians of Aisling have voiced mirrored concerns."

"And rightfully so!" Emery proclaimed. In the dead of night, she leaped into the air, landing with grace on the hardwood. "Doubt and fear are enemies of the strongest warriors and queens, and only the foolish are immune. When there is nowhere else to turn, these demons must be faced with a lethal sword."

CHAPTER FIFTEEN

A week passed before the Gifted children returned to the castle between two forests. The entrance hall crowded with wooden trolleys, which carried the luggage of returning students. An aura of magic lingered in the air. Several professors trailed through the bustling corridors, glancing down at unrolled scrolls. Their wise bits of laughter trailed off in a chorus of welcome.

"Come now, Alice," Emery spoke. "Don't gape like a new student; the others are beginning to stare."

"Oh, there you are!" Juniper pushed through the idle crowd. "I've been searching for both of you. Ariadne and Fionn wait in the common room of Lancaster Hall. To say the least, the other female students are intrigued by the presence of the latter."

"Naturally." Emery sighed with a curious grin. "Fionn is a modest lad, and such attention does not suit his introversion."

"You're not wrong." I chuckled before turning back to Juniper. "Are they waiting for us?"

"Indeed," she huffed. "Follow me."

I raised a single brow as she turned to stride through the hall. A little creature peeked through her tangled curls, looking around with a pair of bulbous eyes. *Peb.* The tarawisp was beginning to shed his thick coat of dandelion fluff. A sharp squeak escaped his mouth as a spark danced across my fingertips. My sister clucked in a soothing manner. When I looked up, the creature had disappeared without a trace.

"Don't scare the poor thing!" Emery pinched my forearm.

A trail of laughter followed us through the castle corridors. It seemed to echo between the walls, harmonizing with the rhythm of our footsteps. The hem of Juniper's gown twirled around her ankles. Several students turned to watch as we passed, but not an ounce of embarrassment weighed on our shoulders.

As we reached Lancaster Hall, the delights of return crashed into the realities of confrontation. I stepped into the candlelight, before following the others toward the loft. The common room was unusually silent. A small group of girls lounged beside the fainting couch as each one whispered between sharp bursts of laughter. I swayed between the bookshelves with anticipation, as the looming conversation promised to address the memories. I didn't care to think about those visions anymore. When all was said and done, I was bound to turn to the headmistress with the unfiltered truth.

"There you are." Ariadne's voice floated between the endless collection of novels. "We've been waiting for ages!"

"It's not a bother," Fionn added with a careful smile. "Patience is a virtue, after all."

"Well then," I responded. "You must have summoned us for a reason. I've noticed the rare, worrisome look settled over your brows. Perhaps you would care to explain."

"I've been thinking." Ariadne sighed.

"An honorable practice." Juniper nodded with a solemn expression.

"We need to share the memories with the headmistress," Ariadne continued. "We cannot keep the truth as a secret. It deserves to be shared with the people of the realm, with those who have lost beloved children and other members of their clans."

My eyes widened and flashed toward the lad. Fionn lounged across a leather chair in the corner of the alcove. A novel flopped open in his outstretched hands while he listened to our conversation with undeniable interest. His gaze was determined, not confused, and this simple fact sent a sudden chill over me.

"She told me," said Fionn, after watching our brows furrow with apprehension.

"Everything," Ariadne admitted.

"Without our consent," I spoke with a hint of bewilderment. "Have you gone mad?"

"He deserves to know," Ariadne retorted.

"Well," Juniper intercepted. "Doesn't everyone deserve to know the truth?"

"Of course," said Emery, "but it must be revealed at the proper moment."

"And when do you suppose that special moment will arrive?" Ariadne inquired, allowing her voice to escape in a tone of defense. Her words seemed to evoke the silence that settled between the bookshelves.

"You can trust in me, as I have placed trust in each of you," Fionn spoke through the tension. "For the latter half of childhood, the faint memories of Saoirse's death haunted the corners of my mind. When the sirens captured me on the shore, a false promise slipped through their lips. They spoke of a reunion with my sister and the other children who gained their wings in that feverous battle. It was impossible, of course. Nothing can separate the innocent from the hands of the Creator; however, the notion imitated a fragile piece of hope. It was enough to lead me into the cavern of dungeons."

The lad spoke without much expression. A pale mask covered the usual tint of his cheeks. His jaw clenched against the tears that pooled around the corners of his eyes.

"Oh, Fionn," I breathed. "You have proven the strength of the human spirit, for the sorrow of loss does not pass without a great deal of pain."

"You are lion-hearted." Juniper nodded.

Fionn looked at me for a moment, searching for something unknown. He gestured toward the mere items

133

and furniture that surrounded us—the old books, soft carpet, and crackling fireplace. "Life is not about getting by here." He sighed, before allowing his hand to rest on his heart. "It is about getting by in here.... My sister does not walk in this realm. She dances in the land of eternal life, in the heavens that birthed the purpose of humanity."

I remained silent, musing over his words.

"You are a strong girl, Alice," Fionn continued. "Unlike so many others, your faith never fails to lead you in the right direction. Some people are destined to be a lighthouse for a lost comrade."

"You must refer to the Lennox clan," I replied in a skeptical tone. "Although the term 'comrade' would not be suitable for the lot of them."

"Perhaps not," Fionn replied. "But I will not be so foolish to assume that you never felt a tinge of compassion for Cleona. As for myself, I pity the lass and her elder brother."

"Her brother?" I inquired.

"Indeed," said Fionn. "I've only just met the lad, but I can assure you that he is nothing like the man who raised him. Cleona was the child to bloom away from her father's sight, yet she has been infused with so many of his terrible vices."

"Cleo cannot survive without the approval of her wretched father," I snapped. "This flaw will be the cause of her downfall."

"Noble is kind," said Ariadne, "like his mother was once."

"Perhaps the memories of her life keep him from falling into darkness," Emery murmured. "As I recall, her spirit seemed to flicker through the halls of the Lennox house."

"There is always light to be found in unexpected places," Juniper recited with a smile.

"And there is always a wee candle to set ablaze." I raised my chin with renewed confidence.

❧❧❧❧

Hawthorne was seated in the leather chair behind her writing desk. Her chin rested in her right palm, while her left hand fiddled with the sleeves of her gown. Countless scrolls and empty jars of ink scattered across the table. A feathered quill stood upright behind her elbow, waiting for the next assignment. Despite the presence of five troublesome students, the old chamber was unchanged since the first time I stood within it.

The headmistress listened to our plea with careful attention. As I spoke about the detailed memories, her brow settled with the horrors of realization. I watched the change in her expression, which shattered at the end of the tale. Her sapphire gaze traveled through turbulent emotions—confusion, anger, sorrow, and regret. It was strange to watch her reaction, for it was nothing akin to my expectations. Words poured from my mouth without hesitation, for the truth was not meant to be caged. When all was said and done, the weight seemed to lift from my shoulders, caught on the wings of an unknown fate.

Zara stared at me, unable to catch the tears that streamed down her face. I watched her search for an answer, until she allowed her shoulders to slump over in exhaustion. She was broken, shattered like glass. Even so, there was something valuable to learn from her expression—women, even the strongest, are not invincible to the emotions of the heart.

"*A chuisle mo chroí.*" Zara's voice cracked in anguish. All at once, her soul seemed to shatter before me. I watched with unease as her shoulders trembled. She remained silent for several moments until a piece of composure returned. "Everyone knows someone who lost a piece of themselves to the epidemic. Few people know the sorrow that it placed on me. In the midst of that feverous plague, my love gained his wings. His death was bitter and unexpected, as the previous week brought our engagement. Kristofer was aware of his affliction, but he did not have the strength to tell me. He was a good man. Perhaps I should've seen it in his eyes, or perhaps the fear of loss prevented me from noticing the warmth that abandoned him. I was frightened, as everyone was. And when I found him on the floor of the castle hall, it was not difficult to blame myself for his death."

"Oh, Zara," I spoke with remorse.

"Please," the headmistress replied. "Do not take pity on me, dear lass. Time has healed the wound, but a scar will always remain. There is no shame in the vulnerable. As for those memories, your grandmother has unveiled the deep roots of deception. Sir Lennox hides in a dangerous place, careful to wear a mask over his forgotten crimes.

The Order of Birch underestimates the man. His allies are more powerful than expected.

"You must remain close during this time, for danger lurks around every corner. I have reason to believe spies walk these corridors. To ensure your protection, Killian will be permitted to enter the castle at his wishes."

"Are you sure?" Emery inquired. "I am not eager to face the backlash of the Lennox clan—or Bastian Amulet, for that matter."

"Well then," Ariadne snapped. "You must squash those fears! A good life is never lived without a bit of risk, and this battle is well worth every one."

"Keep watch, dear girls," Zara interrupted. "The truth will not hide for long. Although you have saved the realm from potential sorrows, the consequences are unknown."

CHAPTER SIXTEEN

I walked across the open meadows, beside walls of purple heather. An autumn breeze plucked at the hem of my gown, ripe with a lack of enthusiasm for the cold. A couple of days had passed since the conversation with the headmistress, and nothing had changed since.

I wandered for the hour, musing over the mere image of my grandmother. She was a kind woman, and there was little reason for her to keep memories as secrets. Nevertheless, her words always seemed to hide significance.

It was not long before a pelt of fur flashed behind the branches. A fox appeared on the edge of the trodden path. "I've been waiting for you," Killian said. "And I must admit you've tested the limit of patience, *cailín rua.*"

"Very well then," I replied with a grin. "You must watch over me, as I stand before you in an unusual place."

"Indeed," Killian responded. "You must understand, Alice. It would be foolish to leave you alone at this time. I am not the only one who watches with the vigilance of a hawk."

As he spoke, the fox glanced around in concern. His amber eyes searched through the blooming heather, while his ears perked forward with the rustle of brambles. He searched for someone in particular, someone whose name wasn't difficult to guess. The hair on my arms stood on end as a flash of movement appeared beside the tree line. Killian was right—someone followed me.

"What does she want?" I questioned.

"Lennox?"

I nodded.

"It's difficult to know for sure," said Killian. "Is Cleona aware of her father's crimes? If so, she stands beside him as an equal and wants this realm to forget about the past."

"I haven't the slightest idea," I whispered, allowing my gaze to trail off toward the woodland.

❧❧❧

That evening arrived with the warmth of fresh bread and candlelight. The dining hall was alive with the festivities of autumn, which promised to end before the new moon. My sister sat across the table accompanied by Juniper and Fionn. Her smile was bright and full of hope, even despite hidden struggles. It was impossible to ignore the glances tossed between her and the fair-haired lad. I wanted to slap both of them into the proper senses.

As I watched their interaction with slight amusement, a familiar figure appeared beside me. He slid into the empty seat as a smile split across his face. He was dressed in an emerald doublet and pair of riding breeches. His boots were splattered with fresh mud.

"Hello, Ronan," I greeted him with a courteous nod. "Riding for the hunt, were you?"

"Indeed," he responded before glancing down at his plate. Without moving a finger, he lifted the teapot and poured the liquid to the brim of his mug. "Care for a replenish?"

I shrugged as the porcelain floated over and poured water into the empty cup. The steam seemed to rise in a careful manner, unsure of what to expect from such tension. It was a simple gesture, of course, and there was nothing to bother about.

Emery stared at me with a peculiar expression, waiting for me to return on a long train of thought. Her smile twitched with amusement, rather akin to my own. A moment passed before I noticed the arm that rested across my shoulders. It was unexpected, affectionate, and everything that belonged to a friend.

But it didn't feel right.

The others were staring at us.

I stood after taking a quick sip of tea. It was far too hot, although nothing burned me.

"I must be off," I announced with a glance of hesitation. "The professors have piled our desks with assignments. I've too much reading and little time to spare."

"So soon, Alice?" said Juniper. "But you'll skip dessert! I believe the chef has prepared fresh tarts and white cocoa."

"Oh, well!" I sighed. "I am sure you can indulge without me."

Ronan looked up with a careful expression, searching mine for something unknown. An uncomfortable frown curved at the edge of his lips.

I strode out of the dining hall and through the open corridors. The faint light of the evening was beginning to fade from the realm. It dappled across the castle walls and bled through the crevice between each stone. My thoughts seemed to race in one thousand directions, although each stemmed from a single moment in time.

What just happened?

I hurried up the stairwell. Both hands clasped over my cheeks, which burned as red as roses.

Was Ronan flirting with me? Has this world turned to madness?

Perhaps I was thinking too much. He was a good friend, after all; friends put their arms around each other all the time. My sister's expression flashed back into mind, prepared to challenge this dismissal. As I reached the top of the stairwell, the image of her smile turned a switch of realization. I found myself musing over the similarities between the way I spoke about Ronan and the way my sister spoke about Fionn. It felt like someone had punched me in the stomach.

"Can one *ever* stop thinking, even just for a moment?" I murmured.

"What troubles you, beastie?"

I turned on my heels to face the fox. His red fur ruffled in an unusual fashion, and his tail twitched with slight agitation.

"What are you doing here?" I asked.

"Oh, must we really go over this again?" Killian groaned. "As you know well, I am the *Guardian* of the Four Elementals."

"No, what you are doing *here*?" I restated. "At this moment, when you could be anywhere else."

"I heard something," Killian replied, "a strange sound, like a distant scream."

Silence fell over the corridors. I stared at the fox for a minute. His pelt spiked with a sudden shiver. There was not a sound to be heard, and the Guardian did not pause to listen. He trotted across the stone floor and turned around the nearest corner.

"Where are you going, Killian?" I demanded.

"Don't speak," he huffed. "Just follow me."

And so I did—through the hushed corridors. All the while, listening, searching for something unknown. At one point, the fox halted and held his muzzle to the ground. His ears flicked back for a moment before he continued forward. I began to recognize this part of the castle, but there was no time to stop and admire the surroundings. Without a word of warning, Killian dashed down a narrow hall with walls that shimmered in the darkness. He stopped in front of a single door and nodded toward the silver handle. He barked with impatience. I glanced down and placed my hands on the door—the entrance to the headmistress's chambers.

My heart skipped a beat at the mere sight of the abandoned place. The study was left in shambles, the desk surrounded with papers of unknown significance. A teacup was shattered across the floor, dotted with specks of blood. A chill swept over my arms as the pieces began to shift into place.

I walked over to the writing desk and examined the letters under the chair. Hawthorne's familiar penmanship was scrawled across the pieces of parchment. A thick scroll was torn across the middle while half waved over the edge of the desk. Few of the documents were related, and no one spoke a hint of her sudden disappearance.

Did the headmistress leave against her own will? From the looks of the broken, blood-splattered porcelain, there was evidence for such a claim. Or perhaps it was her own mistake, an attempt to escape the castle. Either way, there was reason to fear for her protection.

She knew far too much.

My thoughts flashed back to the sighting beside the heather and the words of the headmistress spoken not so long ago. A spy walked the halls of the Academy for Gifted Youth. This student must have learned about our recent conversation then shared the information with the Order of Birch. It wasn't difficult to piece the details together.

As I glanced up from the desk, the fox retreated from the chambers. His red tail streamed through the doorway, while his claws clicked across the floor. Without a word, he left the space behind.

"Killian!" I exclaimed. "Oh, please wait for me."

After taking another look at the scroll, I rolled both pieces into my satchel and rushed after him.

"What do you have to say about that?" I demanded. "And *where* are you going now?"

"With all due respect, dear one," said Killian. "Do you ever stop asking questions?" He halted at the end of the corridor and turned to face me. In his eyes, there was a curious expression—a mixture of fear, anger, and resentment. Although Killian did not know what happened to the headmistress, he was sure of the one responsible. "I must speak with Lachlan and the others," he said. "We must find her before it's too late."

"For what?"

"If Lennox has the heart to murder those Gifted children," said Killian, "there isn't a chance he will hesitate to harm the headmistress."

"Zara isn't defenseless," I snapped. "She could as well be the queen of this castle. Her magic is powerful, and she will not step down from her throne without the loss of battle."

"Oh, I have no doubt," Killian replied. "But it would be foolish to believe one soldier stands a chance against an entire brigade."

"So, what is the plan, General?"

"Gather the troops," Killian barked, "and find the headmistress."

Before I had a chance to protest, the fox disappeared around the corner. Dusk was falling over the castle. The nearest painting on the wall began to dull, as though the colors drifted into slumber. I observed for a moment and turned to hasten in the opposite direction. It wasn't long before I stepped into Lancaster Hall, where Violet and Ariadne studied on the floor of the common room.

"I need to speak with you," I addressed the latter. "*Now.*"

Ariadne closed her field guide with a sigh of defeat. All the while, she seemed relieved to abandon the work. She followed me into the chambers, where Emery and Juniper giggled between gentle gossip. Their eyes flashed to attention as we entered the room.

"Alice," said Emery, "are you all right?"

"No," I breathed. "No, I am not—Zara is gone."

"What do you mean by 'gone'?" Ariadne closed the door with care.

"What happened after you left the dining hall?" Juniper inquired, sitting up from her bed.

"Hawthorne is missing!" I exclaimed. "Her chambers are a mess of torn papers and broken glass. Splattered blood stains the surface of a shattered teacup. And the headmistress has disappeared without a trace."

"Oh, for the love of all that is good!" Emery cried. "Where is the sense in this?"

"I don't know what to think," I whispered, suddenly aware of how I shook with emotion. "Killian has gone to meet with the rest of the Guardians. He's determined to find her soon enough."

"Perhaps the fox will not need to search all the land," Ariadne spoke.

A soft knock sounded on the door, followed by Augusta's voice. "Five minutes until lights out, ladies!"

she spoke in a melodic tone. I listened as her footsteps trailed off into the distance.

I glanced around at the other girls. There was nothing more to tell them. My mind reeled after the scene in the headmistress's study, the drops of blood and shards of glass. I slipped into a nightgown and crawled into bed. A heavy weight leaned on my shoulders, and only sleep promised consolation.

"Can't we do something, anything at all?" Juniper begged. "It is torment to stand and wait for someone else to take action."

"Killian will share the news with the other professors—I am sure of it." I flicked my wrist to extinguish the flame of the lantern. "For now, we must have faith and wait in patience for his return."

CHAPTER SEVENTEEN

When the final hours of darkness fell upon the valley, a strong hand clasped around my mouth, waking me from a deep slumber. I opened my eyes with sudden terror, releasing a muffled scream. Someone was in the room—several people, actually. Against the moonlight, their silhouettes moved around the chamber. Their voices were harsh, although their words seemed to blend with the horror of passing moments. These were strangers, unknown to me. Not of pair of golden eyes loomed in their ranks.

From across the room, I recognized the snow-blonde hair of my sister. She stood with her back toward me, restrained by the hands of an unknown woman.

Juniper stood near me, overcome with sobs and tear-stained anger. Ariadne was beside her, caught in an attempt to fight the silent force of her assailant. Her screams were like roars against the hands of another, as she was unwilling to give up the battle. With a sudden strike in the groin, she knocked the man onto his side. One of the women grabbed her hair before she had a chance to scream.

I searched around in wild panic. With a single movement, the stranger pulled me across the floor and flung me over his shoulders. I thrashed and kicked and protested as my mother instructed her daughters long ago. As I summoned the fire from my core, a burn spread under its touch. It shaped into a scarlet handprint on the man's skin. He shrieked but did not drop me to the ground.

Another stranger approached and locked a pair of bands around my wrists. All connections to the element seemed to fade, as the metal prevented the flames from reaching my fingertips.

As the group piled through the door and moved into the common room, a single figure stood against the moonlight. Her sleek black hair was pulled back in a braid. She remained in silence, raising a single brow as we passed into the corridor. *Cleo.* Her presence ignited a flame of resentment in my soul. That was the last moment before the realm faded into a perfect shade of black.

❧❧

My consciousness returned in the back of a wagon, which traveled over untrodden lands. Both eyes flashed open against the light of the moon. It felt surreal, like nothing more than a nightmare that followed into the waking hours.

I glanced down at my wrists, recognizing the metal bands that imprisoned me. As the wagon bounced once more, I raised my attention to familiar faces. Ariadne and Juniper were huddled on the other side of the cart, murmuring between each other. A pair of guards stood on either side of them. Neither seemed to care much for the conversation, as one nodded off with snores.

I felt a hand rest on my shoulder and glanced back into the face of heartbreak. All silver and white under the light of the moon, her gaze was encircled with purple shadows. Her thin shoulders trembled against perturbation.

"Oh, Emery," I whispered. "Please forgive me."

Without a word, the girl shook her head in response, to assure lack of blame. Her pale hands were bound in the same metals of enchanted restriction. Despite the slimness of our wrists, the bands were impossible to remove. A delicate keyhole was built into the sides.

I dared to analyze the guards for clues to our destination. Neither seemed to notice, as each stared off into the distance. Muffled conversation lingered between them, often separated with periods of silence. I did not recognize their faces, besides the one who towered over the others. He was the armored knight who stood outside the doors of Castle Moss—nothing more than a passing face, not so long ago.

"Where are we going?" Ariadne demanded with her chin raised toward the nearest guard.

He didn't respond.

As we passed through the darkened woods and crossed into the land of white birches, it was not so difficult to guess. I peered through the barred windows of the cart. Silver moonlight poured over the trees while shadows danced across the earth. Castle Moss stood in the distance, with stone rooks that towered over the autumn forest. The horses turned onto a path that led toward the entrance. The wagon pulled around the side of the castle and halted beside an arched stairwell. The knights kicked the doors open and lifted us out into the breath of midnight.

"What are we doing here?" I questioned. "I demand to speak with Amulet—any member of the Order of Birch!"

"Hold your tongue, lass," the female guard warned. "Or the chance will be snatched from you!"

"Do you know *who* we are?" Ariadne spoke despite the orders. "Open your eyes! No matter the orders of Sir Bastian and the Lennox clan, the Elementals have spared this realm from a fate of darkness and desolation."

Ariadne's words did not awaken the senses of the knights. I met her eyes with defeated hope. Without acknowledgement, the guards jostled us across the dew-covered grass, under the stone arches. A large courtyard loomed in the distance, complete with a boundless maze of hedges. The knights pushed us off the path, through a pair of large doors. We stepped into an unknown part of the castle, into halls that smelled of dust and ashes.

"The dungeons," Emery whispered.

She was focused on the stairwell in the distance, where steps spiraled down under the ground. A flicker of light reached out from the shadows. Nevertheless, the guards pushed us forward, toward the candlelight that bloomed in the nearest hall.

The knights locked us in the west wing of the castle, where no person could hear the sound of our whispers. In truth, it was not neglect. The place did not possess a dungeon large enough to contain us, and the rest of the castle was luxurious, even in comparison to the Academy.

We were confined—alone.

I thought to escape through one of the windows, but the ground was far from the second floor. The glass panes did not break against the impact of a vase. I wished to heat the frame and break the boundaries with the force of flames. I looked down at my hands. Those metal bands were a prison for the Gifted soul.

As dawn peeked over the mountainside, a pair of maids delivered a basket of food and fresh clothes. The fine material and buttered rolls looked exquisite—and therefore, unsettling. The servants had kind eyes, although neither spoke a word. Ariadne shoved the basket across the floor. Our stomachs growled with hunger, but we did not dare to eat the food.

The Order of Birch wanted something from the Four Elementals, and the Lennox clan plotted it, without a doubt.

We needed to escape.

But even if we managed to step beyond the western end of the castle, the knights were sure to capture one of us. They stood on all sides, waiting for us to make an attempt. It was useless without a developed plan.

Morning passed into the afternoon, which transformed into the evening. Night came and went in a careless manner, as though the moon cared not about girls hidden behind castle walls. Regret settled in the pit of my stomach. Few people recognized the intentions of the Lennox clan. My grandmother's memories should have been shared in order to reveal the truth.

We slept in a large drawing room, across a cluster of fainting couches. Paintings of unknown figures decorated the walls. The portraits reflected the faint light of the moon, which shone through translucent curtains. Whispers of fear and frustration floated across the chambers. Each one seemed to take on the spirit of a ghost, wandering longer than intended. I closed my eyes and imagined the wisps that carried those thoughts to others.

"What does the Order want from us?" Emery asked. I turned to glance at her in the darkness. She was curled up in a lounge chair, nestled between an assortment of pillows. Tears stained her cheeks, and sobs racked her delicate frame. While the others snored in peace, she rested without slumber, never allowing her gaze to fall. She was a captured horse, a caged bird—tired, hopeless, and longing to be free.

CHAPTER EIGHTEEN

The next few days passed without much change. A pair of maids appeared often, delivering and retrieving baskets. Hunger drove us to eat the food, eventually, and it did not contain a trace of poison. The Order of Birch needed—or wanted—us alive.

I wandered down the corridors, into the final hall before the border of locked doors. The faint perfume of roses wafted through the air, accompanied by the lilt of a voice. I followed these to the entrance of a large hall, where dust and dreams collected in corners.

Alone in the empty ballroom, a wild girl danced across the floor. Her bare feet hurried with graceful steps, which swept her dress into a haze of fabric. As she moved in time with the music, a marvelous voice escaped her lips and transformed into a scream of mixed emotions. She twirled once more, combing her hand through tangled curls. Her gown gathered into a heap as she tumbled to the ground.

"Juniper?"

Pulling her gaze away from the floor, the girl glanced up at me. A stream of tears swelled in her viridescent eyes. She did not seem surprised; rather, her expression held a trace of consolation.

"Oh, Alice," she greeted me. "I must apologize."

"For what?" I inquired.

"Everything," Juniper whispered. "Everything that has happened. I can't help but feel as if the blame rests on my shoulders. If the Creatures had never ambushed the carriage in the Night Oak Forest, our problems would be different."

A single line of gold ran down the lower half of her right iris, away from the deep entrance to her soul. It resembled a single drop of rain, or a stream of watercolor paint. She saw our world in colors that no person could transform into words. She lived with a soul that shone like moonbeams through her character. Everyone seemed to marvel at her presence in life, as she embraced light in the same manner flowers embrace the sunshine.

"Please, Junip," I spoke in a severe voice. "Do not blame yourself for the inevitable trials of this life. We have little control over the things that happen to us. Besides, the matter of fault has nothing to do with it." I gestured to the closed doors beyond the ballroom. "On the contrary, Stone, you are one of my greatest friends

That title is not earned with ease."

"You're much too kind for your own good," Juniper spoke, lifting her face from her hands. "I am grateful for your friendship, more than you know. You have always been such an honest person, unafraid to speak the truth, even when it dares to burn."

"Well, I have faults of my own," I replied with a grim expression.

"As everyone does," said Juniper. "But it's the light that must be acknowledged, don't you think?"

I smiled in agreement, resting in the knowledge that mistakes do not form the true character of an individual. It was the first smile to appear in this chamber of restriction—devoid of virulence and vexation.

"We must escape," Juniper whispered. "Something is wrong, indeed. While time passes, Sir Lennox draws closer to a position of power in the Order of Birch. As we stand here, in this forgotten ballroom, a nefarious plan forms in the mind of another. We must kindle the fire of rebellion in the Gifted." Her expression sharpened with each word of speech. "I will not crumble without a sword in hand."

Mere moments later, footsteps sounded in the corridors. A pair of knights appeared under the arched entrance. "You've been summoned to meet with Sir Bastian Amulet," the stout one grumbled.

Juniper and I shared looks of confusion and slight exasperation. Together, we left the ballroom, before our wrists were bound like those of prisoners. The guards shoved us through the nearest doors, which unlocked with the simple turn of a key. I observed as one of the knights slung it back around the armor on his waist.

Juniper was too focused on the shards of glass in the walls. It was a strange sight, to watch our reflections imitate the movement of candlelight. Our faces warped with each shape, until the entire walk imitated that of a circus. I wanted to step inside the mirrors, to see this realm in a careless, colorful dance.

The knights led us to the entrance hall, where tapestries and portraits lined the walls. Pride swelled beneath my chest, which soon deflated under the weight of the circumstances. A stairwell carried us to the second floor of the castle, where the traditional tartans and artwork did not follow. I remembered these parts, along with our previous call to the castle.

"I don't see the other girls," Juniper whispered to me. "Where are we going, exactly?"

"I have an idea," I replied in a hushed tone, though the guards did not seem to notice.

The knights marched along in formation, while several others joined in passing. Their armor clamored with distinct rhythm. It seemed absurd to wear such attire behind stone walls. Then again, this was a battle of sorts.

As we approached a familiar door, harsh voices drifted underneath. The wood gleamed in a perturbed shade of scarlet. A flood of warped light poured through the entrance. It swung open without a single touch.

"Ah, ladies," Bastian spoke from behind a large desk in the center of the room. "We've been waiting for your arrival."

My heart dared to break away from my chest, pounding louder than ever before. Emery and Ariadne sat in front of the writing desk, each with their backs toward me. Several members of the Order of Birch wandered around the chambers, engrossed in hushed conversation.

Juniper looked at me with a blank expression. The knights shoved us forward and shut the doors. Shadows engulfed corners of the room, where strangers lingered in observation. Their brows raised at the sight of us, as though our appearance did not meet their expectations.

"Please," Bastian spoke again, "take a seat beside your comrades."

And so we did.

"I must admit the castle maids keep wondrous accommodation, even despite the confined quarters." My voice broke through the silence that followed. "Let us skip over the masked introductions, shall we? What do you want from us, really?"

"Well, Hanley," the man replied. "One should expect that short-tempered disposition—the orange hair reveals all."

"It's *ginger*," I snapped, though he seemed all the more amused.

"You ask me to get to the point," Bastian continued. "And so I shall. We have reason to suspect each of you are involved in a secretive plot with the Guardians of Aisling. Such behavior acts against the laws of this establishment. As you know well enough, the Guardians have been reduced to minimal association with the Order of Birch."

"And that gives you reason to snatch four students from their chambers in the darkness of night?" Ariadne questioned. "I am sure you've gone mad—"

"Who shared these suspicions with you?" I glared at the man, hinting for my friend to hold her tongue.

"That question shall remain unanswered," Amulet replied. He opened a thick piece of text on the desk in front of him. "Now, let's set about solving this matter. Your late grandmother, Orinthia, once stood in this position in the Order of Birch. She was quite influential and well-respected, although her methods and morals are unsuitable for these times. The realm does not remain in a rigid, unchanging state. As time moves on, so do the Gifted people, as myths and legends serve little purpose."

"Unsuitable for these times?" Emery repeated his words with astonishment. "By the standards of whom?"

"My grandmother wasn't well-respected," I corrected him. "She *is* well-respected, and always shall be. She cannot be replaced with a feeble character, nor anyone in this realm of good and evil."

The man furrowed his brow and leaned back in his chair. He stroked his beard with a thoughtful, trite expression. The other officials gathered close, listening to our interrogation with sudden interest.

"Enough with this!" A sharp voice spoke from the crowd. A dark-haired man stepped forward before locking his eyes on mine. "My patience continues to wear thin."

Lennox.

A scoundrel, murderer of hundreds. He stood in the shadows of the room, amongst the most influential in the realm, like a man deserving of the highest honor. His gaze did not waver from mine, although it held the slightest trace of prudence. His eyes were black, like those of his daughter, and nothing like those of his son.

My thoughts flashed back to the conversation overheard beside the gardens, the harsh words exchanged between Cleona and her father. The latter valued the unattainable, a realm of common people, without distinction between powers. He did not see the beauty of rarities, the unique traits that blend into a single race. He believed in an age-old falsehood, the lies of an ancient foe. Peculiarities coursed through his veins, as the blood of the Lennox clan was not so common after all.

A burst of outrage leaped from my heart, taking the form of an amber flame. It vanished without the chance to take flight. For all the men, women, and children to perish under the darkness of another, a flicker of hope remained.

Bastian gaped from across the desk. He didn't know the truth—no one did. Like the others who paused in a moment of fear, the man was fascinated with the strength of my fire. Even as I turned to glance at my sister, she stared back in surprise.

"Where is Professor Hawthorne?" Ariadne dared to break through the fearsome silence. "Have you shared a sort of ransom notice with our parents?"

"Nonsense!" Bastian shook his head. "No need to speak in such a manner! Investigation has revealed the exchange of confidential information, through the form of materialized memories. Hawthorne is suspended from her duties at the Academy until she complies with rightful interrogation," Bastian continued as the knights appeared beside us. "We know who was involved in this matter, ladies, but the content of the memories remains unknown to all besides the receivers. You must share the memories with us. You have a duty to this realm, like all others in it."

"You're quite right," I responded after the silence that followed his words. "Although I am not sure where your loyalties rest—with the Gifted people, or the manipulative actions of a certain individual."

Bastian fiddled with the feathers of his quill, which dripped with the blood of unspoken words. I watched the crease deepen across his forehead. His mouth dropped into a slight frown.

"You have no idea," I murmured, allowing the tears to fall with freedom. I gestured to the gathering that surrounded us. "None of these people know the truth—the truth of the shadows that have plagued this land. You don't know the Lennox clan. If anyone did, they'd fall under the weight of it, cursed with the nightmares that creep into dawn."

"What do you mean, lass?" an old woman spoke from the group of strangers. Her eyes were gentle, like those of a grandmother; her silver lashes fluttered with concern. She ventured down the dangerous path of oblivion, and there was little time to turn around.

"The Lennox clan is responsible for the rebirth of the Creatures of the Night Oak Forest, as well as the fatal fever that swept over the villages." My fragile voice overpowered the rise in commotion, while an internal flame began to melt the bands around my wrists. The knights did not take notice, as each one focused on Lennox and Amulet. "He traded poison with the witch of the forest, and poured it into the wells. Hundreds of Gifted men, women, and children passed under his allegiance to the warped morals that have scarred this realm. My grandmother hid the truth in her memories, left behind in a stain of ink. She sought to protect the Gifted people, to save the value of this life and all the uncertainties that come with it."

As the final word escaped my lips, the enchantments broke away from my arms. A fire ignited in my hands, spreading down to the tips of my fingers. I pointed toward the cold-faced man. Lennox did not flinch against the threat of accusations, even as the others searched his expression.

No one spoke for a several moments, which stretched out into the thunderous silence. Lack of words dared to shatter the glass windows, to extinguish the flames of chandeliers. A shiver traveled over my shoulders, like the whisper of an unseen spirit.

"I told you once, and I shall once more," Lennox huffed in a manner of dismissal. "The poor lass has succumbed to madness. This interrogation is a waste of precious time."

"Oh, the wicked fools!" Ariadne cursed under her breath.

"A mere hundred years ago, these children would've hung out in the gallows for their conspiracies," Lennox stated. "It is a matter of treason."

"You're wrong, sir," Juniper spoke over the crowd of Gifted officials. "And I've never met one as clever as she."

"Ah, yes," Lennox clucked in a sympathetic tone. "The tangled one is the worst of the bunch. Although I suppose she takes after her father—an attack from the Creatures was sure to mess with the imaginative workings of the mind."

"As a matter of course!" Ariadne laughed aloud in bitterness. "I suppose your son was not the last child to suffer under the painting of a false portrait."

"Enough of this!" the elder spoke up once more, stepping close to the writing desk. "I believe it would be foolish to disregard the claims of these fair maidens. Do not sweep the surface with an idle hand. You should consider their words with care, Sir Bastian, as the Elementals once saved this realm from oblivion."

The man did not speak for a long time. He scratched his beard with a far-off expression, as his gaze traveled over each of our faces. There was something unbreakable behind his eyes. He snapped his fingers with sudden force, and the knights stepped forward to seize our arms.

"What is going on?" I demanded. "Now where are you taking us?"

"Back to the western end of the castle." Bastian sighed whilst tapping his fingers on the wood. "I've grown tired of this conversation. The gathering will benefit from an intermission. According to the postman, a letter has arrived from Macnas Manor, addressed in part to the Hanley twins."

Before we had the chance to speak another word, the Elementals were pushed into the corridors, snatched from the final trace of hope.

CHAPTER NINETEEN

ays passed without another word from the Order of Birch. I felt like a caged phoenix, eager to spread my wings and glide far away from confinement. For the worst part, an unbearable separation existed between the castle walls, as news failed to reach the western edge of the castle. A letter from home acknowledged our disappearance, but each word failed to hint at the state of things.

I kept watch at the windows, in careful search of the tree line, where neither fox nor archer appeared to me. I wished to see the students and professors of the Academy for Gifted Youth, to watch their wonder climb high as the week continued.

My thoughts remained with Ronan, Kade, and Fionn. *Did they know the truth—the brutal, unfiltered truth?* A trickle of remorse seeped through my veins. I read over the letter from Macnas Manor in order to distract from the emotion.

My dearest girls,

Hold tight to the courage in your hearts. Your parents continue to pray and plead for your release with each moment. We hope this letter reaches you without restraint.

The Guardians have called to the manor, though the fox was not among their ranks. Perhaps you have seen him through the windows of Castle Moss? He watches over you.

Lachlan spoke of the memories your grandmother left in her wake. Anguish has filled my spirit. Several days ago, the knights appeared on our doorstep, with several others from the Order of Birch. Your father does not trust the Lennox clan. His suspicions are rightful, to be sure.

The O'Reilly twins visited this morning, along with Fionn MacMillan. When I opened the door, each demanded to know where you have gone. Ronan was quite upset, as you should know, and all the students are in an uproar over the absence of the headmistress. The truth is difficult to understand.

Have courage, dear girls.
We shall see each other soon.
Le grá,
Mama

I folded the letter back into the pocket of my night-gown. A storm brewed on the edge of the horizon, cracking across the night skies. Raindrops began to batter the windows of the old castle.

"Alice!" Emery's voice called in the distance. "Oh, *where* have you wandered?"

I stood up and called out in response. Despite the confined quarters, it wasn't difficult to get lost between the identical chambers. Reflections of candlelight swept through the open doors. My sister appeared with a lantern in hand.

"Where did you find that?" I questioned.

The knights did not permit unwatched flames behind these doors. A sort of fear grounded this restriction. And so, the darkness of night was unbroken.

"If I told you," said Emery, "I'm not sure you would believe me."

I glanced up with hesitation. An unfamiliar sort of excitement danced behind her eyes. For the first time in weeks, a trace of hope was there, with the truth that refused to remain hidden.

"Tell me," I insisted. "Now you must!"

Emery held a finger to her lips. She retreated down the hall in silence. She paused after a few steps, prompting me to follow in haste.

The corridor was alight with the glow of flames. Each shadow leaped with the grace of a dancer, interrupted by the brilliance of the lantern. There was magnificence in the fire, the same element that breathed from the mouths of dragons. It was a beacon in the chambers of eternal darkness.

We turned around the nearest corner, where a thin blanket of dust covered the floors. Unknown spirits stared out from framed portraits. Their lifeless expressions revealed nothing to me.

The other girls appeared soon enough. With a swing of the lantern, their faces glowed in candlelight. A set of troubled expressions plagued their brows. This side of the castle did not have much to keep captive teenagers entertained. Without the use of our powers, the isolation was akin to punishment. There was little to speak about, and far too much to think about.

"Did you tell her?" Ariadne demanded.

"What?"

Emery halted in front of a stone wall. She looked straight ahead, with blue eyes unbroken. An ancient tapestry hung over the cobblestone. There wasn't much to observe. It was akin to the other walls that lined the rest of the corridors.

Emery did not shift from her place or respond to the conversation. I watched her pull back the fabric to reveal a looking glass. Her reflection stared back with a careful expression. She raised one hand and touched her fingers to the mirror. A ripple spread across the glass, before the wall contracted and opened with a slide of the stone. I stepped forward in astonishment and stared down into the passage. It extended far into the distance. A row of torches lined the narrow path, while the hook of a lantern protruded above our heads.

I stared onward with a blank expression, while the others observed in amusement. A swift burst of laughter escaped in place of the words that refused to part from me.

"Where do you suppose it leads?" Juniper inquired. "It would be shameful to march through those cobwebs, if only to find ourselves in the walls of the dungeon."

"Well then," I replied in thought. "A maze of passages runs under the Academy for Gifted Youth. The entrances are scattered throughout the castle, and few students have managed to gain access. Lennox is one exception. It would not be foolish to assume the tunnels extend to Castle Moss. That would explain the night she left after curfew."

"Of course!" Juniper exclaimed.

"Killian seemed to think she snuck out into the forest," I added. "It makes perfect sense. In the hope of her father's approval, she reported us to the Order of Birch."

"Oh, that *witch*!" Ariadne scoffed.

Emery hushed the girl before turning to face me. There was the hope again. It seemed to shine from the depths of her gaze—all silver and blue in the light of the moon.

"We must leave this place," she whispered. "Once again, the fate of Aisling depends on us. These secrets cannot be kept from the Gifted realm."

"You're right." I sighed. "But we mustn't leave tonight. It would be foolish to trek through the woods without direction. Where can we find shelter? As soon as the knights notice our escape, search parties will flood the villages."

"Oh, brilliant!" said Ariadne. "We cannot step into our own homes. Too obvious. Macnas Manor will be subject to a raid—no doubt."

"We need a plan," Juniper affirmed. "Let the night pass without a care. We'll leave at the next sign of dusk, and nightfall will spoil their chase."

"Clever one," Ariadne quipped. "I'd love to hear the rest of that plan."

"In the works," Juniper replied with a grin.

CHAPTER TWENTY

Morning arrived in a careful manner, as though the sun hesitated. It covered the drawing room in a blanket of golden light. I glanced up after rubbing the traces of slumber from my eyes. The others slept on the fainting couch. It was uncomfortable, to be sure, but it didn't seem to matter.

Somewhere between the corridors, a grandfather clock spoke in solemn tones. I wanted to hear his words, to greet the newborn hour with him. There was wonder to be found in the rhythmic clang of the bell.

I recalled the nights of a restless girl in the middle of winter—candlelight, snowfall, and warm biscuits. She didn't seem so far from the present moment, from the freckled maiden behind the looking glass. Her character remained a phantom of childhood spirit. Her voice returned every so often, with words of the surreal sort.

I slipped out of bed and stepped toward the windows. I pulled back the curtains and gazed out into the lands beyond, where a flash of movement caught my attention. A layer of fog covered the hedge maze beside the old gardens. Statues reached through the clouds, while a figure appeared in their midst.

That woman walked toward the castle each morning, with a massive bouquet of wild roses in hand. She never failed to arrive after the first light of dawn. I mused over the delight of such a job, even despite the corruption it served. The lass was able to support herself through the most romantic flowers in the realm. I observed as she handed a single rose to the knight at the gatehouse. He accepted with a gentle nod before lifting the blossom to his nose. She passed through the entrance without restriction.

"Flowers are such glorious creatures," Juniper spoke from behind me. "A single bud can awaken the realm from a bitter season. It's much like the power of friendship."

"I suppose you're right," I replied with a faint smile. "Although that doesn't provide much consolation at this moment."

"What troubles you, Alice?" Juniper appeared beside the window frame. Her fingers fiddled to release her mane from a loose plait.

"Nothing more than the unknown." I sighed. "The future taunts like a child."

"There will come a time when you remember all the little worries and realize that few held true worth," said

171

ERIN FORBES

Juniper. "You are a bright star in the darkness, connected to a constellation of light and hope. My dear friend, allow your life to unfold."

I glanced back at the girl. She was unable to hide the anxieties that plagued her mind, but she never allowed such fear to control her actions. There was something to learn from her courage.

"Have we found our heading?" Ariadne spoke, rising from the couch in a single sweep. Her eyes were alight with anticipation.

"Not quite," I responded. "No one knows where the passage ends. If it leads outside the castle, we will be most fortunate, but we are sure to lose direction otherwise. A course of escape will depend on the location of the mouth."

"Well then, there is nothing to lose." Emery appeared beside me. "Either conclusion outmatches the lack of hope in this castle."

Her words preceded the faint sound of footsteps in the corridor. In a matter of seconds, the chamber fell into silence. Closer and closer—the steps approached. The strides were soft, unlike those of the knights. I shifted back from the glass and turned toward the open doors. The other girls mimicked these actions and stood beside me.

A moment passed before the figure appeared against the shadows. She was familiar, even for a moment; my heart dared to leap with faith. *Professor Hawthorne. Could it be?* The woman stepped into the light. It was impossible to mistake that dark hair and sapphire gaze, which the maid did not possess in features.

172

"Mornin', ladies!" She wheeled a silver cart into the room. Platters of pastries covered the surface, with pitchers of juice and plates of the unknown. "Breakfast is served."

"Hello, Elsie," Ariadne greeted the lass with a vapid expression.

"Ah, now," the maid replied. "Don't be so miserable, miss. It's sure to improve soon enough, with the shift of command down in the kitchens. There'll be baskets of fresh scones before the week ends!"

"Contrariwise, I am concerned with matters of greater significance than a few fresh pastries." Ariadne rolled her eyes.

"Very well then." The maid sighed with a glance at the rest of us. She brushed off her apron and retreated into the corridors.

"I cannot survive another night in this prison," Ariadne snapped as the woman disappeared. She pulled on the metal around her wrists, which bore patches of blistered skin. I watched her fists clench in outrage before she released an infuriated scream. That sound echoed across the western end of the castle; it resonated into the final hours of daylight.

❦❦❦

I stood beside the windows once more. A blanket of light settled over the distant meadows. I found a trace of hope there. A strange sense of anticipation invaded me. I watched as the sun hid behind the trees, casting long shadows over the land.

Several hours remained before the time of our departure. A detailed plan mapped out in our minds, with alternative paths into the coming night. A flow of adrenaline rushed through my veins. It ignited a single flame, which dared to awaken the heart of more than one individual.

"We'll be all right, Alice," Emery spoke from behind me. I glanced back to meet her gaze. A plait of fair hair curved over her shoulders.

"How can you be sure?" I whispered. "One can never be sure."

"I am quite certain," Emery replied. She stepped toward the glass, as her eyes shifted toward the first star of the evening. "Courage and faith are devoted sisters, in the words of our father. We must focus on the constellations, for the true power reigns beyond. Those rare children did not pass in vain. If the knights capture us, the realm will not crumble in a matter of moments. We are destined for more than this prison."

"We have stepped into a dangerous game," I shattered the silence after her words. "I've considered the threats to our lives, and I am most fearful for those who follow us. Sir Lennox has murdered hundreds of innocents. His daughter is ruthless, clever, and desperate for acceptance. Our families and friends are nothing more than a few additions to their list of undesirables. The headmistress is detained in the dungeons; to be sure, several others are there as well. Each moment spent behind these castle walls, is valuable—and bound to the hands of consequence."

"That hidden passage is a gift from the heavens," Emery murmured. "I hope it leads a path to the forest."

I glanced back toward the glass, which caught a glimpse of our reflections. My hair shone like a flame against the candlelight of the chambers. It sparked with the sudden shout that bounced between the corridors. My sister turned with widened eyes before gathering the hem of her gown. The shouts did not cease. Without a moment's hesitation, we strode across the room and rushed down the shadowed halls. As we approached, the voices hushed, and a group of familiar figures appeared.

"Oh, Alice!" Juniper exclaimed. She turned on her heels with a look of astonishment. "You will not believe the sight!"

And she was right.

A pair of lads stood before me—one fair and the other freckled. Their shoulders were covered in dust and cobwebs, though their smiles stretched wide.

"Your Majesties," said Ronan, "the noble rescuers have arrived." His deep blue eyes settled on mine. We stared at each other for a moment, until I noticed the open passage behind him. The others shifted against a delicate silence.

"You're not quite the epitome of knights in shining armor," Emery spoke, unable to hide her amusement.

"You saved my life once before," Fionn responded. "I have come to return the favor."

"How did you find the passageways?" I questioned. "This entrance has been sealed for ages. I am sure it isn't marked on the maps of the system."

"Believe it or not, the task wasn't too difficult," said Fionn. "After the dormitories were searched, the little guardian appeared. He's full o' wit, that ginger one."

"I was determined to find you—to steal you away from this wretched place," said Ronan. "It isn't rightful. The Order of Birch has no reason for what they've done."

"You should not have come here," I spoke in a wavering voice. "It's too dangerous! You don't know the trials we have endured behind these walls. Armed knights stand behind each door, keeping us like the cursed bands around our wrists. If we manage to escape together, it will be the work of providence."

"Self-confidence is admirable, Alice," said Juniper. "But that doesn't mean you shouldn't accept the help of friends."

"You always feel the need to be strong, red," said Ronan. "It's exhausting! For once in your life, allow someone to carry you through the gunfire."

I looked up from the ground to meet his gaze. There was something there, familiar and unexpected. Despite his tone of voice, a soft blend of happiness and amusement spread across his lips. His smile teetered over the edge, prepared to break into a bit of laughter. I wanted to shut his mouth with my hand, and laugh with him at the same time.

"Where is Killian, by the by?" Emery raised a single eyebrow at me. "I thought he would've been the one to find us."

"The fox waits in the forest," Fionn replied. "There are far too many spies around. It would be foolish to send him—much too predictable. Ronan volunteered to take his place, and I followed after the gallant lad."

"Of course!" Ariadne sighed.

"The troops await, dear ones," said Ronan. He glanced back toward the passage, which extended far under-ground. "There is not a moment to spare!"

"Oh." Juniper looked forward with wide eyes of emerald. "It's so dark in there."

"Not as darkened as this castle," said Ronan. "I'd walk both with a lantern in hand."

With that, the lad stepped into the shadows, and the others followed after him. I did not glance back into the corridors. As the entrance closed behind us, I listened for the shouts bound to break above our heads. Flickering candlelight guided a path through dust and cobwebs. A narrow staircase continued down to level ground.

"You're safe," Ronan assured, "for the moment, at least. Even after the knights realize you've gone, the passages remain hidden."

"He's right," said Ariadne. "Although I doubt the lot will waste much time in search of the tunnels. Once we've escaped, their plot dares to crumble. Lennox and Amulet will set out with the hounds, to be sure."

"Well then," I spoke. "So be it!"

We trudged onward for a while. My skin crawled against the cool air. The narrow passage provided little room for comfortable conversation.

CHAPTER TWENTY-ONE

We reached the end of the passage as the moon brightened the skies. Silver beams shone upon our cheeks, pink and freckled in the light. There was warmth, even despite the breath of winter.

"Just as we left it," said Ronan. He pushed open the trap door under the roots of an enormous tree. A thick layer of moss covered the wood. Each branch reached through the earth, in search of the unknown. After shutting it back up, the lads covered the entrance with leaves and thistles. Under the shadows of the roots, the passage hid in plain sight.

As I stepped into the night, the voices arrived—shouts of order and anger, somewhere in the distance. It wasn't difficult to imagine the sight of wild horses and armored knights. Their sounds echoed across the woodland.

"Where are we?" I asked. "I don't recognize these parts."

"The Night Oak Forest," Ronan responded. "Not far from the border of birches."

"How strange," Juniper murmured. "It feels so different."

"What do you mean?" I inquired.

Juniper placed her hands upon the nearest tree. Her gaze flashed with a trace of sadness, which covered the fears beneath. The low branches shuddered against her touch, awakening from a sort of depression. Juniper closed her eyes and listened with a furrowed brow. Her cheeks were paler than usual, sullen with the weight of knowledge. I watched in silence as the wind carried the leaves over her shoulders. Her nightgown resembled a ghost in the darkness.

"She hears the whispers," the girl told me. "Each word speaks of blood and poison."

I staggered back and glanced at the bands around my arms. For a moment, a familiar girl returned to mind, with ginger curls and scented candlelight. She feared the flames under her skin, the power that surged through her spirit. She spoke a warning to me. This was a dangerous game, without the chance to turn back.

We strode down an untrodden path, which continued toward the white trees in the distance. My fingertips sparked with embers, which brightened the shadows that extended onward.

"Are you afraid?" Ronan whispered.

"No," I replied in a soft tone. I focused on the ground, where the ashes of autumn spread under our boots. "As a child, I feared the woods, but much time has passed since then. The forest has grown roots in my heart, found a home in my soul. Each tree is a kindred spirit, an everlasting friend."

Ronan looked at me for a moment. His gaze was careful and attentive. "I was not referring to the forest," he said. "Are you not fearful of the future, the uncertain fate that plagues this realm?"

"Perhaps," I responded. "Nothing is certain in this life; there is little sense in fear of the inevitable. We fight for the things that must change, and pray for matters beyond our control."

"And which do you suppose this falls under?"

"Both."

We exchanged a glance of hesitation before the lad strode ahead. In that fleeting moment, a million questions came to mind.

"Ronan, wait!" I placed a hand on his shoulder in order to keep pace. "Where does this path lead? You always seem to know where you're going, and I haven't the slightest notion."

"This is an undeclared battle," Ariadne interrupted. The dead grass swayed as she skipped toward us. A dismal cloud of fog separated in her wake. "Let us hope *an púca* doesn't come around."

"Excuse me?"

"*An púca*!" Ariadne laughed. "Come now, Alice! You must know the tale of the spirit that wanders these lands.

The shapeshifting creature arrives in times such as these to warn of grave danger and haunt those of falsehood. For some, his character is a sinister one; for others, *an púca* brings good fortune."

"I've heard one or two tales of the sort," I replied with an unamused expression.

"A band of gypsies once chased my mare through the moorlands." Ronan chuckled. "Each one was convinced her golden eyes and dark coat were the surest marks of the *púca*."

"Do you really believe in such tales?" Emery asked.

"Why not?" Ariadne questioned. "We are living in one, to be sure!" She strode toward the front of the group, even as she did not know where to turn.

"Ronan," I addressed him with a sigh. "You haven't answered the question. Where are you leading us?"

"Ah, I see you haven't changed!" he replied with a mischievous smile. "You are an impatient one. You'll have to wait and see!"

I glared at him.

"Trust," Ronan said. "It's a glorious notion!"

And with that, the lad strode forward with amusement and slight satisfaction. My sister replaced him. Her pale eyes glimmered with a blend of emotions.

"He's ridiculous," I murmured in a harsh tone.

"Ronan seeks to gain your trust," Emery responded. "And it's never granted with ease."

"If such words spoke truth, a sensible man would share the name of our destination!" I snapped. "He's acting like a child."

"To catch sight of your smile," she hummed. "Must you be so oblivious, Alice?"

"I am no such thing!"

❧❦❧

An hour passed before the Gifted students halted beside a road marker. A pole stood in the center of the forgotten path, complete with wooden arrows pointing in each direction. The paint was worn from lack of maintenance, and the remaining words spoke a familiar yet foreign tongue.

Fionn halted beside the marker and revealed a puzzled expression. After a moment, he pointed straight ahead. "This way," he spoke, allowing his words to draw out in hesitation. He examined a broken compass in the other hand.

"No, that's not right," said Ronan. He raised an eyebrow at the unbalanced piece of metal. "We must head northwest."

"Oh, no," Fionn groaned. "That route will lead straight to the entrance of Castle Moss. You're thinking in circles, Ronan."

"Are we lost?" Juniper inquired. She stood with a collection of autumn leaves in hand.

"It would seem so," Ariadne huffed.

"Ye're *both* wrong!" a gruff voice spoke from behind us. I spun around to greet a familiar forest troll. "Follow the western path, and that'll lead ye straight to the edge of the forest. Ye best make haste! Those old knights aren't far off ye're tracks."

"Willoughby!" I greeted the creature. "What are you doing out here?"

"I *was* searching for lionberries," Willoughby replied with a slight roll of his eyes. "At the moment, I am speaking to ye!"

"Are the knights in search of the girls?" Fionn asked the troll.

"Well, I'd say so!" he responded before sticking his nose in the air. "And I'd say they be lookin' for the lads as well! What with all the ruckus around that old castle!"

"Does he know?" I whispered to Ronan.

"O' course!" Willoughby snapped. "Ye can't keep secrets from me! I've got eyes and ears around all corners of the woodlands."

"Half the realm has received word of the truth," Fionn commented. "It's a mere matter of who believes it."

"Shameful be those who don't!" Willoughby exclaimed. "They be supporters of the Lennox man himself!"

"It's a miracle my grandmother managed to survive with such a weight on her shoulders." My voice drifted against the winds of winter. "Even so, rumors spread like wildfire. It can be difficult to recognize the truth when spoken from a man without evidence."

"Ah, life... 'tis a difficult battle to fight," said Willoughby, "but the beautiful moments will always make up for the sorrow."

A soft wind rustled through the treetops, carrying the cold song of the season. The troll buttoned the moss coat around his torso. I caught sight of the first snowflakes to fall over the land.

"Did you hear that?" Ariadne spoke suddenly.

"What?" Several responded in unison.

The petite girl stumbled back for a moment, holding her fingers against her temples. She closed her gray eyes in concentration. All the while, a light breeze floated through the forest. It brushed against our ears, as if the earth longed to share a secret. Ariadne glanced up with a change in expression.

"We need to leave," she whispered. "*Now.*"

"What's wrong, lass?" Willoughby glanced around in bewilderment.

"The knights are coming!" Ariadne gasped. "They're riding on horseback, led by the nose of their best hound. If they find us, we're dead—as good as pirates hung in the gallows. They're not far from this path, and that dog will lead them straight toward us."

I looked into her eyes for a moment, into the deep patterns of steel. The wind carried whispers, along with the melodies of winter. It spoke to her without hesitation.

"Bless your Gift, Moss!" Ronan exclaimed. "We must leave this place at once."

I glanced down at the troll, who stood with a crease between his brows. "You mustn't tell anyone we've passed through here," I told him.

"As a matter of course, my dear!" Willoughby responded. "Upon my word! I'd dare not perish in the flames of such treason."

"Thank you," I replied.

With a swift nod of his head, the plump creature retreated into the undergrowth. I glanced at the others before we continued through the darkened woods. We trekked onward into the night, until our heels formed blisters against the backs of our boots. Some time passed before the moon shone over a ridge in the distance. My flames flickered against the wind.

Ronan removed his coat and handed it over to me. He did not give me a chance to protest as he stepped forward. "The Highlands," he murmured. His eyes focused on the mountains far ahead. "My father used to tell stories about the unfamiliar territories—full of dragons and fallen starlight, peculiar people with brilliant traditions."

"No time to daydream, Ronan," Fionn interrupted. "We're almost there. The theatre is not far from here."

"The theatre?" Ariadne questioned. "So, you're taking us out to a drama! The ballet, perhaps?"

The lads glanced at each other for a moment before their gazes settled upon us. A secret lingered between them. I was sure of it. Ariadne was swift to speak words of wit, but there was not a trace of amusement in the eyes of others.

We walked to the edge of the faded path. A stream gurgled amongst the wildflowers. Ronan strode forward to reach the edge of the grass, where he kneeled down to place his hands against the current. He stood up after a moment and pointed downstream. "This way," Ronan murmured.

My apprehension teemed on the edge of consciousness. It dared to spill over in the form of flames. As the others hurried forward, I stood back and listened. Those armed voices moved close—endless commands of indecipherable intent.

Without a second thought, I marched to the fron
of the line and ignited a pair of flames in hand. Thos
restrictive bands melted in a matter of moments. M
stare burned in the embers of determination. "Stop!"
snapped. "And do not take another step until someon
tells me where this untrodden path leads."

Fionn held his hands over his head. His blue eye
widened like the oceans. Even so, his expression was no
so fearful. The mere sight was fraught with amusement

Ronan turned to me with a slight grin. His gaz
danced with laughter, while those familiar dimple
creased beside his lips. He lowered his chin in consid
eration. "Well then," Ronan whispered. "Walk beside me
if you will. Our destination is not far from here, wher
proper shelter awaits. If you care to wander alone, th
knights are sure to reach these parts soon enough."

I nodded in silence. The flames dimmed to light ou
footsteps. A trickle of laughter escaped the other girls
Ariadne elbowed my sister in the side, while she flashe
an expected glance.

CHAPTER TWENTY-TWO

White birches parted to reveal a ragged hollow in the heart of the forest. An old structure was settled in the center, adorned with flowering vines. The place was reminiscent of a medieval theatre, with rounded walls, weathered paint, and the core open to starlight. It dwelled with the essence of forgotten memories.

From the outside, the place was devoid of human presence—not a soul appeared to the senses. I approached the entrance with reluctance. My arms burned with apprehension, with the fire that flowed under my freckled skin.

Fionn and Ronan walked through the doors, while the others followed in their footsteps. Chipped paint of every color peeled from the interior walls. Costumes littered the back of the stage, providing fresh fabric for curious faeries. Voices of the past seemed to send an echo across the music hall, as though the final production never quite finished.

"Welcome to the Fortress of the Gifted," said Ronan. "The troops await their rightful commanders."

I glanced at him, unable to hide the puzzled twitch of my face. Ronan looked back with all the solemnity expected of a man. I started at the sight of a figure behind him. "Watch out!" I shouted. With no sign of concern, the lad turned around.

The strange character stepped into the faded light of the moon. A quiver of arrows gleamed against his waist. His rugged face and crested coat pulled the trigger of reassurance.

"Lachlan," I greeted the archer with exclamation. "You scared the life out of me!"

The man chuckled as he looked upon us. "Follow me," said Lachlan. "A friend has been waiting for your arrival."

As we walked through the abandoned corridors, voices began to emerge from the silence. Perhaps the theatre was not entirely deserted, and perhaps we were not lone warriors in battle. Between the scattered papers and chipped paint, a distinct promise lingered.

Lachlan led the group down spiraling stairs. All the while, questions poured from my lips, like tea from a steaming kettle. A faint light flickered in the space below us. As we reached the final steps, the man turned to gesture for silence.

I lifted my focus to a wondrous sight. A gathering of warriors rested before me—students, faeries, and creatures unknown. While the performances ended long ago, the Fortress continued to shelter the hopes, sorrows, and dreams of the Gifted. Familiar and foreign faces greeted me with smiles and solemn nods. Each one held a look of renewed hope, returned from a tired frown of betrayal.

The archer led us through, into a small room behind the stage. Dusted tapestries hung over lines between the walls, and old trunks overflowed with costumes around our feet. It was a fine blend of the elegant and haunted. Moonlight trickled through a crack in the ceiling, shining upon a familiar face.

As Lachlan cleared his throat, the stranger lifted his gaze. Noble Lennox was nothing like the rest of his strange clan. Although the boy possessed the bold eyebrows and dark gaze of his sister, his olive skin was a contrast to the pale complexion of his father. It was evident that the teenager had inherited most of his mother's traits.

"Ah," Noble greeted us with a sincere smile. "You must be the four maidens I've heard so much about. It is such a pleasure to make your acquaintance."

"The feeling is mutual," Ariadne responded, failing to hide an expression that suggested otherwise. She did not trust this fellow, and I couldn't blame her for such feelings of apprehension.

After all, the lad was one of them. He was a member of the Lennox clan, raised in the same household as Cleona. Even so, he did not resemble his father in the slightest.

189

His face beamed with the golden rays of the setting sun. His features were akin to the faded photographs of his late mother. It was clear that his temperament derived from her as well.

"Well then," I huffed. "What *are* you doing here?"

"Oh, I must apologize!" Noble said. "I forget that few words have been spoken between us. Indeed, this must be a peculiar experience! According to our spies, these weeks have brought an imitation of unlawful imprisonment. Please, never think of that man before me—that man who does not deserve the title of a father, to anyone, much less his unfortunate children!"

"I don't understand," Emery murmured.

"I stand on your side," said Noble, "to speak in simple terms."

Lachlan nodded toward me in confidence. There was not a doubt in his mind—the mind of a usual skeptic. I raised an eyebrow in response, and the archer sighed with exasperation.

"Look," said Lachlan, "I know it seems strange. Noble deserves your trust more than anyone in this fortress—in this entire realm, for that matter! Like each of you, he is one of our greatest weapons. He knows his father better than anyone, even Cleona!"

I turned to the subject with a hard stare. His brown eyes met mine with equal, unwavering spirit. Intentions are impossible to determine without knowledge of the heart. Noble Lennox was a stranger to me, but he proved to be our best chance.

"Speak the truth," I said. "What's going on?"

Noble stood up from his chair and walked across the floor with slow strides. His shoulders were strong, like those of an experienced soldier. He moved closer, closer to me. His attention seemed to drown in a sea of thought, before snapping back with sudden force. "This is a great battle," Noble replied. "And it must be recognized as such—or the realm shall perish with ignorance."

"Your parents are safe," Lachlan spoke after a minute of silence. "No harm will come to them. Both remain in the comfort of Macnas Manor, under the watch and protection of the finest warriors."

"We must see them," Emery demanded.

"I'm sure that will have to wait." I nodded. "Knights have flooded the woodlands, and there's not a chance of safe passage. At present, the truth must be shared."

"Very well," said Lachlan. "I can see the infinite number of questions that turn in your mind."

"What's happened at the Academy?" Ariadne demanded. "Professor Hawthorne is confined for interrogation at Castle Moss. To be sure, she did not allow those bandits to snatch four students from the dormitories."

"With the blink of an eye, this realm has transformed in the darkness of chaos," Noble said. "Much has been veiled from the rest of the Gifted, as the Order of Birch seeks to avoid revolution."

"Sir Bastian Amulet ordered the knights to take each of you from the castle," Lachlan explained. "Upon learning of this, Hawthorne addressed the man, and he warned against her interference. Of course, she pushed against his orders."

"Sir Barrington works in her place, with the assistance of the elder professors," Noble added. "The lot manages to keep the students in order, and classes run as usual. Behind those walls, few students know the scale of the conflict that rises beyond."

"And the professors have learned about this place?" My focus trailed over the ruins around us. "It must be ancient."

"Of course," Noble said. "It used to be a theatre for the creative arts, a place to share magic with inspired souls. Over the past fifty years, it has fallen into abandonment. After a narrow escape from Lennox Manor, these walls gave shelter to me. Father looks upon the place with disdain, with hatred toward the rarities that once shared their passions with the realm. It's safe—a place he will never send the knights to explore."

"You're confident," Ariadne remarked.

"Indeed," Noble replied. "One cannot conquer in battle without a firm stance."

"And what is your father's stance?" I replied.

"On simple terms," said Noble, "he seeks to rule over this realm."

"For what reason?" said Ariadne. "For centuries, the Gifted people have lived without a monarch. All matters of politics are managed within the Order of Birch."

"These words are more than true," Noble affirmed. "Nevertheless, not all truths rest upon the surface. My father has long since been obsessed with our linage. I'm sure you've heard the rumors that circulate these villages—the Lennox clan descends from a historic stain upon the Gifted society."

"Of course!" I sighed. "Those tales are nothing more than fables."

"The Order of Birch wants the Gifted people to believe so," Noble replied. "Even so, the truth does not fall far from the fable."

CHAPTER TWENTY-THREE

We wandered through the corridors without a destination in mind. The Guardians guided the path, introducing us to each of the individuals that passed. Strangers smiled and waved in response. The elders carried grim expressions, overshadowed by the youthful excitement of battle.

"Over the next few days, each of you will be expected to converse with Noble and collaborate with the rest of the Guardians," said Lachlan. "For now, it will do well to settle into this environment. It's far from the expectations and luxuries known to students of the Academy for Gifted Youth."

Ronan and Fionn trailed off into the crowd, while the archer stared forward in concentration. It was not difficult to see the worries that turned in his mind. I thought back to the fulfillment of the first prophecy, to the care that he directed toward the headmistress and her students. Lachlan watched over the battle with the Creatures of the Night Oak Forest. Upon the dismissal of the Guardians, he continued to protect the Gifted children. As Killian was a friend to me, the archer was more than a friend to the headmistress.

"Do not fear for her," I whispered. "Zara is stronger than she seems."

Lachlan looked back at me with an unreadable expression. It remained for several moments before breaking into a smile. "You're much too clever for your own good, lass."

"You're a strong man with a stern face and kind heart," I replied, "but you're not so difficult to read."

Lachlan laughed. His eyes brimmed with tears of the unknown sort. "I cannot say the same for you," he said. "And I am sure that freckled lad would agree."

"*Ronan*?"

"Of course," said Lachlan. "You've got him wrapped around your finger, for heaven's sake!"

My cheeks burned crimson under the faded light of the moon. "Don't be foolish!" I said. "He's nothing more than a kindred spirit and kind-hearted friend."

"Very well." Lachlan sighed. "But you should know that such friendships are bound to bloom."

The warrior shrugged the gear over his back and stroked his beard in amusement. His eyes gleamed with a bit of wit and careful knowledge. Lachlan brought the lads out of the Academy for Gifted Youth; therefore, he was sure to be close with them. My mind reeled with the suggestion behind his words. Ronan O'Reilly—*fond* of me? How was I supposed to believe that? As a matter of course, there were suspicions. It was all in good fun, and not so very serious.

"We meet again, freckled one."

From the midst of the crowd, a red creature appeared to me. He trotted with ears perked forward.

"Killian!" I greeted him. "You did all this?" I gestured to the band of Gifted warriors.

"With the help of many others," the fox replied behind a curled smile.

"*Go raibh míle maith agat.*" I curtsied with a gentle nod, thanking him in his native tongue. "You've no idea how much your loyalties mean to me."

"Your father has arrived," Killian spoke after a moment. "He wishes to speak with you… alone."

I glanced over at my sister, who looked back with a blank expression. She shrugged and nodded in silence.

"Follow me." Killian's gaze flickered between each of us. His russet tail swished as he turned around. I followed him down the corridors, leaving the others behind.

Several minutes passed before we reached an arched passage, which led to a narrow stairwell. Stone walls followed me down the steps, marked with the shadows of flames. A small hearth greeted me at the end, where my father rested in a broken chair. His gaze lifted at the sight of me. Not a single word escaped him as his hands lifted to his face.

"Father," I whispered. "You're here."

"Alice." He rushed forward to embrace me. "You're safe."

"I've the Guardians to thank for that."

"I have something to tell you, dear one," the man spoke in an unwavering tone. "You must listen with care. I'll speak with your sister soon enough, though one must process thoughts in their own time."

I crossed the floor to sit beside him. His eyes flickered with a hint of hesitation. He was dressed in a fine coat and pair of breeches, but his boots were covered in mud. I couldn't imagine the strides he had taken to arrive at the theatre. A safe route was difficult to find, with the mounted knights that roamed the forest.

"Tell me."

"Your grandmother loved her clan with a steadfast heart," my father began. "She looked upon her grand-daughters with that fierce adoration. Like many others, she never spoke much about her powers. With the time of unrest, it was wise to keep such details behind closed doors. Knowledge holds power—and danger, too. Orinthia recognized this truth and kept her Gift a secret.

"At the age of eleven, I discovered the truth, even as she did not seek to share it with me. Your grandfather and I held it close to our hearts, for the woman was our greatest treasure.

"Years passed on, and I don't believe she ever realized. It didn't matter much to me; there was no need to speak of it. When twin daughters arrived to the house of her son, she looked upon the clan with vigilance. Your grandmother had a sort of sixth sense for matters of the near future. As you know well, there are few Gifted with more than a single power. I often wonder if she happened to be so fortunate."

Listening to his words, I clutched the pendant around my collarbone. The prophetic note remained inside in the vial, secured with a simple string.

"She left this life without a final farewell," Father continued. "As you remember well enough, we received word of her death soon afterward. This preceded the first manifestation of her granddaughters' elemental powers. When those flames caught life in your hands, a piece of her spirit transferred within them. You see, the woman was Gifted with the rarest, most powerful combination of fire and ice. She left this realm without sight of the inheritance that remained. Those flames formed with your creation, but the connections did not surface until the proper moment. Each person is different, each one unique."

"Each lives with a Gift, unknown to another with spirit planted on this earth," I recited. An iridescent tear escaped me. It streamed down to land on the surface of my palm before evaporating against the warmth. "You mean to tell me that she left the elements to us?"

"I like to believe so." My father smiled.

CHAPTER TWENTY-FOUR

"If souls were colors, mine would be blue," said Juniper. She gazed at the sky with a far-off expression. "Not the sad kind, but the thoughtful sort."

"When my hair turns silver and white," said Ariadne, "the color will begin to match my spirit. Nothing compares to the sight and scent of the wind."

We lounged outside the Fortress, along the edge of the tree line. A week had passed since our rescue from the castle, and the search parties had moved away from these parts of the woodland. Snow covered the ground in a cold blanket, which Emery adored more than the essence of freedom. She gathered the snowflakes in her hands and crafted the most wondrous creations. A blanket of frost spread out to trace the silhouettes of guardian angels. It wrapped around the bark of the nearest sycamore. Icicles formed under the branches, clicking together with the sound of windchimes.

"*Tá an aimsir go hálainn*," Killian murmured. "This winter reminds me of the Highlands, the place where I was born and raised. At this time of season, snow falls often, and the mountains are crowned in icicles."

"Tell me more about the Highlands," I replied. "I am curious to know about the people there."

"Very well," said Killian. "The mountains are home to a large number of the Gifted. They're nothing at all like those in the valleys of this realm. They're untamable, wild creatures, with souls of courage and might. Their love for each other is unconditional, and their protective nature derives from this truth. Outsiders are seldom received with open arms."

"True warriors at heart." Juniper nodded. "My grandparents come from their land."

"Perhaps the Highlanders can help us!" Emery said. "We cannot fight this battle alone. It will do well to find more allies."

"What do you suppose?" I turned back to the fox.

"We'll send a letter to a clan that is close with the headmistress," Killian spoke after a short pause. "I'm sure the lot will care to hear about her imprisonment. Assistance is sure to arrive soon after word reaches them."

"Zara knows those in the Highlands?" Ariadne responded with a bit of surprise.

"Hawthorne is wise to keep her friends close," said Killian. "The Highlanders are never afraid to prove their loyalties."

"Very well then," I said. "Send a messenger on horse-back, and be sure the rider is shadowed. Lennox will have knights on the lookout, without a doubt."

"Of course." Killian nodded.

I turned my gaze toward the northern lands, where the trees faded into rough meadows. Streams flowed down from the mountains, as each collected in the white mist of falls. A thick cloud of fog moved over the rocks. Beyond this landscape, the realm was a ruthless and wild place. It flourished like a foreign kingdom, far from the rule of the Order of Birch. In that distance, a light of hope remained.

"Alice!"

Ronan O'Reilly rounded the edge of the old theatre. His sharp voice sent a shiver over me. A pile of frozen petals littered the earth around his boots. His expression dared to fall into a state of panic.

"Come with me," said Ronan. "Quick, all of you!" He grabbed my hand and led me into the theatre.

"What's happened?" I demanded. "Tell me at once!"

Ronan did not speak another word. Killian rushed ahead, not without an impatient flick of his tail. The others followed him in haste.

We turned another corner before the door that led down to the hearth. It was slightly ajar, as a group of children listened in careful silence. At the sight of us, each of them stepped back in shame.

"Oh, Alice!" Kade flung the door open in bewilderment. "Thank goodness! Come down at once. A messenger has arrived from the White Birch Forest. There is grave news!"

I followed the winged girl down to the fireplace, where a band of warriors waited in patience.

"We have received word from the spies at Castle Moss... Sir Bastian Amulet is dead," Lachlan announced. "No one is sure of the cause, though some believe the poor man was poisoned."

"Of course," Emery huffed. "Lennox must be responsible. It makes perfect sense."

"She's right," said Noble. "My father murdered with the intent to take his place as the head of the Order of Birch. Without the interference of headmistress, such plans are bound to succeed. His thirst for power is lethal. It isn't foolish to assume he used the same poison that erased half of the Gifted rarities in this realm."

"Tell them, Noble," Killian snapped. "The truth must be heard."

The fox began to lose his temper, as the depths of his gaze struggled to remain in the preferred form. His eyes narrowed in concentration, while his ears flicked back and forth.

"What haven't you told me?" I demanded.

"The fact of the matter," said Killian, "what Lennox seeks to gain through the success of his infiltration."

"My father seeks power, as you know well." Noble sighed. "He will do anything to obtain it. His sights have long since been set on the throne of this realm. Traced back far enough, our linage leads to one of the High Kings of Aisling, the eldest son of the first Gifted maiden. Almost half of the population descends from the High Kings—far in the distance, of course. My father believes these circumstances provide him with a rightful claim to the crown abandoned long ago."

"*Fadó fadó*," Killian spoke with digression.

"That's madness!" I replied.

"Even so," said Ariadne, "the man's logic isn't entirely off the rails. It presents a decent argument for the foolish."

"Our ancestor was the eldest of five sons, the heir to the kingdom," Noble continued. "That old ruler was banished for crimes of treason. His throne was distributed in fair representation, with rulers from each corner of the realm. His brothers reformed the kingdom with the sacred elements of freedom. Upon their death, the Order of Birch formed to preserve such morals. A hunger for control did not exist. All ambition was satisfied with the leadership of the appointed."

"A state of peace has remained much longer than anticipated," Killian said.

"Sir Lennox cannot believe the Gifted will allow him to assume the throne," I stated. "His sins have come to the surface."

"Yes," Noble replied. "But one must understand that his followers are not weak and bound to wait for the approval of foes. Few have heard the rumors of his crimes, and even less regard such tales as more than tittle-tattle. Where's the evidence, one might ask? In the memories of the deceased, the visions that cannot be seen without the Gift of the local loon!

"My father doesn't fear the bloodshed of innocents," Noble continued. "His ambitions stem from the unknown. I spent the first decade of life with him, unable to decipher the menace that turns with a switch. His temper is unbearable. Others are obstacles in his path. Some can be used as an advantage, while others are bound to be discarded for the cause. While his reason isn't entirely sound, the man is clever—so clever that it strikes fear into the hearts of his enemies."

"What's the solution, then?" Ariadne snapped. "We did not escape his grasp for nothing! I will not stand back and allow that beast to conquer over this realm."

"You are the perfect weapons against his foolish beliefs," said Lachlan. His fingers ran over the feathers of an arrow.

"Why do you suppose my father *despises* the Hanley clan?" Noble replied. "For what reason did he lock each of you inside that old castle?"

A distinct silence blanketed the conversation. I stared at the lad with a hard expression. His gaze did not waver with the beam that tickled the corners of his mouth.

"You are the rightful heirs to the throne," Noble whispered. "The truth is written in the stars, and no one can change it."

"The Four Elementals are destined to take their place as the High Queens of Aisling," Killian confirmed.

The world seemed to fade in and out of focus, darkened at the edge of sight. Ronan's hand settled across my shoulders to keep me from stumbling into shock. His words did not register in my mind. I stared onward for several moments, convinced of a blunder in explanation.

"The families of Hanley, Stone, and Moss," Lachlan proclaimed, "are direct descendants of Ó hÁinle, Ó

Clochartaigh, and Ó Maolmhóna. Orinthia knew this all too well, and the protection of the clans was her sole objective."

"What on earth are you talking about?" Ariadne demanded.

"The ruling clans of the ancient realm," Ronan explained. "As you might recall from several chapters in history class."

"*Queens*?" I choked out the word. "As in rulers over the entire realm? You're out of your minds!"

"Oh, dear." Noble blinked. "I did not anticipate this sort of reaction."

"How long have you kept this secret?" Emery spoke as her fingertips covered with frost.

"To speak the truth," said Noble, "Hawthorne and the Guardians were assigned to this matter ages before your arrival to the realm. It is stitched into the hearts of your families, passed down through the generations."

"Why didn't you tell us?" Ariadne demanded.

"I've been waiting for the proper moment," said Killian.

"*The proper moment?*" I gasped. "I'd care to know when that will arrive!"

"We must take back our kingdom," said Noble. "You're the final hope for the Gifted, the spark in a newborn revolution. My father will fight for his place as the king of this realm. His wicked morals are far beyond the sort to keep peace."

I turned to look at the other girls. My sister stood motionless, with distinct apprehension laced between her lashes. Ariadne looked on with a raised eyebrow, as if she expected the tale to fall into deception.

"I know this seems unbelievable," said Lachlan. "You must realize this has been our plan for months. It's written in the ancient laws of the realm. When the government falls into the hands of the people, the rulers must be chosen from the founding clans. Prophetic notions are not enough to convince the Gifted, but the actions of the Elementals have proven their loyalties to the realm."

"Orinthia was able to see into the near future." Noble retrieved a slim parcel from his coat, before sliding it over to me. "She knew this all along, through each moment spent with you. She transcribed these visions for safe-keeping, in hope that her words might guide the actions of her granddaughters."

My thoughts drifted to the image of that woman—starry eyes, silver hair, and unspoken humor. She wanted this for me, for the people of this realm. She had faith in my abilities, in the decisions of her granddaughters. Even as she passed into the next life, her spirit remained kindred.

"What about Cleo?"

Juniper looked around with a far-off expression. The tarawisp peeked out from her curls, wiggling his mischievous nose. His white coat was beginning to shed, as each seed took flight on the slightest breeze.

"She will stand beside her father, even as far as his intentions place her life on the stake." Noble sighed. "If his work is successful, she will assume the role of a princess, and her darkest wishes will come true. With such control, the Lennox clan will demand the exile and execution of rarities. Our heads will be taken without much time to waste."

"You're saying that the lives of the Gifted people rest in our decision to light the fire of this rebellion?"

"Precisely," said Noble. I watched his face with close attention. His expression was like a steel sword, unafraid to slash his enemies.

CHAPTER TWENTY-FIVE

I strode down the corridors in a slight haze. Strands of hair began to catch aflame, as each tangled piece floated above my head. The embers wrapped my shoulders in a blanket of comfort. Each footstep brought me further from the inevitable.

"Alice, wait!" a strong voice called after me. *Ronan.* His boots crunched against the rubble on the ground. "Listen to me, please! You cannot run from this."

"No, Ronan," I said. "I understand that more than anyone. Allow me a moment to think for myself."

"Fine, then come with me," the lad replied. "You've been stuck in this place for ages. A clear mind can be found on the back of a horse, within the heart of a forest."

"Are you mad?" I responded. "The knights are sure to find us."

"I know a place where no one goes," Ronan spoke in a soft tone. His blue eyes dared to pull me into the wilderness, all for the fear of facing it alone.

"I've missed you," I told him. It was a simple set of words, a truth that had been ignored for weeks. All this time, his dimpled grin was a light to lead me through the shadows.

"You are more of a princess than Lennox proves to be," said Ronan. His gaze darkened in a moment of thought.

"How do you know?" I questioned. "I am nothing more than a girl in the shoes of the chosen one. I am seventeen years old—not wise enough to accept the role of a princess, let alone a high queen!"

"I know," said Ronan, "because your soul shines with the goodness, truth, and beauty of our world. There is starlight and fire in your veins. Those constellations were formed by the hands of the one who created this realm. He created you, too, and all others who live to defend the light of our world."

I stopped at the end of the hall and turned to face him. "This battle does not come as a surprise," I whispered. "It has loomed on the horizon for some time. I did not expect to be the one sounding the trumpets."

"One never does," Ronan replied with a sympathetic expression. "Nevertheless, the music awakens the best in this realm. You are more than capable of leading these warriors into battle, for you are more than a warrior at heart."

Ronan stepped forward with hesitation. He was close enough for me to notice the slightest shift of his gaze. I flinched as a russet tail weaved between our boots.

"Have the two of you finished flirting?" Killian inquired. "There are important matters to discuss, and I am a fox of little patience."

A trickle of laughter fell between my lips. It echoed across the corridors, settling into the shadowed corners. All at once, the world seemed to shift into focus. My heart dared to leap from its cage. Ronan bowed his head in respect and left me to speak with the Guardian.

A terrible moment of silence lingered between words of unspoken worth. Amidst this, there was the distant sound of blades against iron. Each stroke sent a shiver across my arms, as each one sharpened the weapons of war.

Killian stared at me with an unreadable expression. He did not allow his golden gaze to waver. I found the courage to meet it. With a flick of his tail, the fox turned to lead me down the darkened corridors.

"Wait, Killian." I halted before double doors. "Please, listen to me. I cannot be expected to make this decision in haste. You ask me to lead these people into battle, to be crowned with a role discarded long ago. This realm doesn't seek a ruler; it seeks renewal and justice for the innocent lives taken far too soon."

"I agree with the lad," Killian said. "You must step outside of this abandoned place, take a ride through the woodlands. It will nourish your spirit and allow some time for you to muse over the matter."

I frowned in response.

"Lachlan retrieved that chestnut mare from Macnas Manor," the fox whispered. A crease of desperation formed across his brow.

"Fine," I responded. "I'll ride into the forest for an hour… under one condition."

The Guardian rolled his eyes and waited for a response.

"I shall ride alone," I said. "Without a band of Guardians to trail behind, without your presence to lurk in the brambles."

"No, Alice!" Killian lifted his head in outrage. His ears perked forward with a startled look, while his tail flicked around in a single motion. "I cannot allow it. The knights have moved onward, but armed spies lurk around each corner of this realm. Such action would be reckless, and far too dangerous to take the risk."

"You will allow it," I said. "I am not foolish enough to lead myself down a treacherous path. With such a fire as mine, any band of ambushers would fall under a lethal hand. Arm me with a suitable bow and quiver of arrows, if you must!"

After much discussion, the fox allowed me to take off on horseback—not without a pair of sheathed blades secured against both boots. My ginger hair was covered with a heavy cloak, with protection from snowfall and unwanted sight. The material was a dull shade of brown, like that of an average forager in the woodland.

I leaped into the saddle and glanced back at the old theatre. From the outside, it was not so remarkable. Shattered windows and peeled paint, broken beams and rusted metals. Even so, the walls were crowned in emerald vines, which continued to bloom against the breath of winter.

❧❦❧

White birches reached over the untrodden path. Cantering hoofbeats carried me forward, far from the expectations of others. A stream of tears flowed against the frozen air of the season. I pressed the horse onward, unwilling to give in to the emotions. The trees passed in a faded haze. Each dark eye stood out against its trunk.

What is wrong with me?

Everyone dreams of this sort of revelation. It reminded me of a novel, a childhood tale of fiction brought to life. Even so, the mere thought dared to tear me apart.

At the age of thirteen, the truth of my origins and elemental powers was enough to send me into a crisis. Four years later, a strange lad told me to assume the throne of a long-lost queen.

Alice Alexandria Hanley—High Queen of Aisling. Keeper of the flames. Ruler of the Gifted realm.

I tugged on the reins and allowed the mare to slow to her stride. I wanted to escape the future, to return to those summer months of solitude. It was peaceful then, under the warmth of the sun. There was laughter in the meadows, under the light of the silver moon. The weight of anticipation replaced all of these notions.

Felicity strode down the hillside, toward the snow-covered moorland. Chilled air nipped at the bare skin around my gloves. A willow stood in the near distance, cloaked in branches of beaded ice. As much as it swayed, the tree did not move from its place in the ground. Its roots held tight to the earth with determination.

I rode through the moors for a while, until the skies settled in shades of pink and gold. The throne did not leave my mind, even for a single moment. I halted on the edge of a cliffside, which overlooked the expanse of the birch forest. A stone castle peeked out from the center, reaching over the white branches. It was strange to think of the darkness that moved behind its walls.

As I turned to ride back, a flash of movement caught my attention. I stood up in the saddle and shielded my eyes from the sun. My heart dared to skip a beat. A group of mounted horses galloped across the glen, each one headed toward me. The cloaked riders remained unrecognizable, with heads covered in black hoods. I pushed the fire back into place, remembering the pair of daggers strung below my knees. A million possibilities trailed through my mind.

"Who goes there?" I spoke in a gruff tone to mask my own.

"Three fair maidens of honorable intention," a familiar voice replied as the riders reached the ridgeline. Their heavy strides slowed to a swift halt. I noticed the silver crests on their saddle blankets. The lead figure lifted their hood to reveal a fair countenance.

"Emery?"

"See!" Ariadne chuffed before lifting her cloak as well. "She hasn't thrown all sense to the wind."

"We've come to speak with you," Juniper said, "to make sense of all these wild notions."

"Ah, yes! You must refer to the matter of the throne," I replied with a slight frown. "The highest position in the land, which has been placed on the shoulders of four teenagers!"

213

"It seems like madness," Emery spoke in concentration. Her fingers combed through the mane of her horse. "Yet it would be foolish to dismiss it as much."

"We shall not be the first young women to claim such positions of power," said Ariadne. "The nations of that land beyond the portal provide several fine examples. Some of the greatest rulers have accepted their role before two decades of life."

"Aisling depends on us, once again," Juniper murmured. "Our fears have nothing to do with the matter."

I glanced between each of the girls—kindred spirits beyond compare. All together, we were ladies of the same age and similar circumstances, the High Queens of the Gifted realm. We did not ask for this position. The stars aligned to present it to us.

"I cannot survive this alone." I sighed.

"You shall never be without friends," Emery reminded me. "Darkness cannot be faced without the union of light."

"Lift your chin, Alice! Our fate is not so terrible after all," said Ariadne. "You seem to forget that a queen does not rule alone."

"We shall be the voice of the Gifted people," Juniper spoke in a gentle tone. "The Order of Birch must be cleansed of its sins. Once she is rescued from the castle, the headmistress will guide and stand beside us."

"My life has transformed into an old fable," I said. "I am a stranger to this world—and nothing seems real."

"This realm may be strange, but you are no stranger," Ariadne snapped. "You've found a moment to breathe— now gather your senses!"

"Oh, hush!" I replied. "Mere hours have passed, and the entire band of warriors expects to hear of a decision."

"Come now, Alice," Juniper spoke. "You must know that we do not seek to pressure your choice. This matter deserves thorough consideration, for the sake of your happiness and that of the kingdom. At first, our reactions were quite akin to your own."

"How did you settle upon it?" I inquired, avoiding the strength of their stares.

"I learned to consider the welfare of this land," Juniper responded. "And I found the happiness of the Gifted to align with my own."

"We must acknowledge the truth," said Emery. "Without our claim to the throne, the realm will fall under the power of the Order of Birch. Sir Amulet has been poisoned at the hands of the Lennox clan. An age-old secret has come to surface in the form of a legend. It must be recognized as a true stain upon history; the people must work to prevent its repetition. I will not sit back and watch it happen on our account."

I lifted my head to gaze at each of them. Ariadne was seated astride her mount, with reins clutched tight between her fingers. The other girls were seated in proper side saddles, each of which appeared to be entirely uncomfortable.

"Will you stand beside me?"

"Always."

CHAPTER TWENTY-SIX

S everal days passed without much time to rest. Most afternoons were spent in conference with the Guardians. As we waited for word to return from the Highlands, archers kept watch over the villages. I was permitted to ride through the forest, so long as the red fox followed.

"Have you made your decision?" Killian asked one evening in the woodlands.

"Indeed," I replied in a brisk tone. "I shall speak with Noble and the Guardians tonight."

"And would you care to share your answer with me?" Killian inquired.

"Perhaps," I said. "You must promise to not regard it with amusement and self-satisfaction."

"Upon my word." The fox trotted after me with a curled grin.

"Well then." I sighed. "Yes."

"*Gabh mo leithscéal?*"

"Yes," I repeated. "I shall accept the crown that fate has presented to me."

Killian looked up with wide eyes. His expression was not too difficult to read. While this matter had been pushed to the back of discussion, the choice was made several days ago. Noble continued to pester for the final decision, and I held it close for some time. It is never wise to speak in haste.

My parents visited the night beforehand. Their guidance did not attempt to shift me. Even so, it carried news that boiled the blood in my veins.

A group of knights raided the manor over the weekend, and there was nothing to be done. My father was out on the town when the riders arrived at the doorsteps. Mother gathered herself with courage, though the men did not listen to her refusal upon entering the household.

What was there to search for? Evidence, one could assume. Some writings that might speak of the Hanley twins and their strange connection to a deceased relative.

Macnas Manor was fortunate to remain intact, despite a few torn documents and mud-stained carpets. On the other hand, anger burned in the heart of my father. He refused to leave his wife alone, conscious of what might've been. In such times of trial, his protective nature was not to be discarded. It was rooted in his devotion to kinship.

The knights left with news of missing horses and unremarkable chambers. Not one discovered the hidden bookshelves and passages under the floorboards.

"Have you ever thought to run away from it all?" I asked in a far-off voice. Notions of enchantment seemed to weave around each word. "It's a wonder to think about... for even a moment, at least. I'd like to climb aboard an old ship and sail out into the bay—far enough to wander, never far enough to stray."

Killian stared toward the distant mountains, without a single point of focus. "I suppose," he responded. "Many years ago, I wanted to return to that den in the Highlands—the place where my litter was raised. I wandered without purpose. I lived in the heart of the Night Oak Forest, and I watched it crumble under the weight of the curse. My sense of belonging was torn apart after the death of a brother. I sought to return to the familiar land, and soon realized that it would never be the same—even after my return. It was sure to be a ghost of those memories, nothing like the original.

"Kristofer Ó Coileáin approached to inquire about my interest in the work of the Guardians. At the time, the fellow was positioned as the head archer. Lachlan was an apprentice out of the Academy for Gifted Youth. Before he succumbed to the fever, Kristofer was an honorable man with his entire life ahead of him. He pulled me out of the darkest hours, and I found renewed strength as a Guardian of Aisling.

"Once upon a time, I thought to leave it all behind," said Killian. "I never think like that these days, as this land has become a true home to me. It wouldn't feel right. After all, I am bound to these emerald fields and forests."

The fox glanced at me with a stern expression. He strode onward without another word. I followed, while the echo of his tale remained.

We wandered for some time before the earth swept down to the banks of a stream. My horse pawed at the ground, with both ears perked in anticipation. Killian trotted forward to take a drink from the waters. Giant sycamores towered overhead, naked in the bitter wind. Smooth rocks protruded from the brook, as the footpath continued to the other side. It was a familiar place that sparked memories of summertime.

"Where are we?" I asked the fox. "I recognize this place."

At that moment, an eerie figure emerged from the undergrowth. Wild waves of buttercream curls flowed down her back. A delicate crown perched on her head. Her dress was torn and covered in the blood of an unknown creature. She was not so much a ruler on the surface. Her anxious eyes resembled those of an ordinary child.

Killian glanced up from the stream and startled at the horrific scene. A small group of black bears stepped out from behind the girl. Those massive beasts trudged forward with heavy paws. Each of their heads bowed with sullen expression.

"Clara!" I gasped. "What happened to you?"

"He's gone," the child whispered. "The knights have slain him."

I slipped out of the saddle and approached with hesitation. For once, the band of bears did not seem concerned.

"His blood rests on my hands," Clara murmured. "He suffered to protect me from harm."

"Dear one, listen to me with care," Killian spoke in a gentle voice. "You must tell us what happened. Whose blood covers your hands?"

The girl looked up with sudden realization, as though she hadn't noticed our presence until then. A flood of relief washed over her face before she sighed with a broken expression. Clara rushed forward and fell into my embrace. A single tear streamed down her cheek. She whispered a word of foreign language—the name of a friend.

"The knights," she whispered. "A band arrived at dawn and sought to take me back to that old castle. Their leader spoke about finding a 'proper home' for me. The bears tried to fight them off! One of the armored men unsheathed a dagger and pierced the heart of the alpha. I watched him bleed out across the earth. I tried hard to keep him here. I wanted to keep him with me! The effort was useless. One cannot cheat the angel of death, even when it arrives without notice."

"Oh, Clara." My chest burned with the flames of anger and compassion. "I do not have the words to mend a broken heart."

"No one understands," Clara murmured. Her voice cracked in a distraught tone. "This birch forest is my rightful home—each tree, freckled bough, and drop of water. My little fingers contain more strength than the hearts of ten misguided men."

I held the little queen in my arms, and placed her in the saddle behind me. The bears watched in silence as their breath clouded against the frost. A feeling of dread settled at my core. It called for a certain kind of change.

At the sound of my voice, the horse cantered onward. Her hoofbeats slammed into the frozen ground. With a firm sense of direction, the mare dashed over the trail. Sunlight swirled through the white branches, collecting in thin wisps on the breeze. Each ray settled down upon the snow-covered land.

We rode down a sharp ridge, which gathered into a hollow of moss. The distant bellow of hounds swept over the woodland. Each sound stirred the anxieties in my heart. It was an awful thought, to have an entire realm depend on the decisions of four teenage girls.

There was far too much to consider at once.

"What troubles you, Alice?" Clara inquired. "Your hair sparks with embers. I can hear the worries on your breath. Each one radiates from the core."

"Nothing of your concern," I replied with a sigh. "You must know the fears that wander a mind of loneliness. Courage is not so simple to harness."

"Oh, I wouldn't worry so much," said Clara. "If ever you find yourself in a situation such as mine, find comfort in the world that surrounds you. Nature—in second place to love—is one of the greatest gifts we have been given."

CHAPTER TWENTY-SEVEN

When we arrived, the Fortress came to life. People of all ages rushed around the derelict place. Not one seemed to notice the pair of girls covered in blood and flames. Their conversations blended in a smooth hum, much like that of a disturbed beehive.

I dismounted and handed the reins to a stern-faced groom. Lachlan and Noble stood at the entrance of the theatre. Their gazes settled upon us with sudden interest. I approached in hesitation, with one hand clasped around that of the fair-haired child. She whispered a few words to her bears before each of the beasts wandered off into the forest.

"I have far too much to tell you," I spoke to the men.

"I can see that," said Noble. "For now, it will have to wait. Our guests have arrived from the Highlands...

accompanied by the headmistress of the Academy for Gifted Youth."

The lad waved a hand over his shoulder in a casual manner. A pair of elder maidens greeted Clara with the warmth of open arms. The little queen glanced back for a moment before she was ushered down the corridors.

"When did she arrive?" I demanded. "I must speak with her at once."

"She waits besides the hearth," said Lachlan. "The others are there as well."

Without another word, I lifted my hem and sprinted through the shadows of the old hall. My footsteps echoed across the theatre. A group of warriors turned to watch as I passed without a second glance in their direction.

"Alice, wait!" Killian's sharp voice called behind me. "You must slow down! You have no idea what conditions the woman has suffered. Her appearance may come as a shock to you."

I halted in front of the narrow staircase. The fox nipped at my heels in irritation. I glared at him in silence before descending the stairwell. Voices and firelight trailed up the steps. I listened with care as the conversation hushed. The sound of footsteps preceded my entrance to the hearth room. It was a small space, packed with people of all sorts.

"Professor Hawthorne," I called as the crowd turned to face me.

The Highlanders spoke in a thick brogue, which reminded me of the elders in the Stone clan. Their eyelids shimmered with the golden dust that could be found in the center of a rare flower. Patterned freckles dotted their complexions—white as snow and dark as night. Most watched behind pale eyes, and several gleamed with the colors of transformation. Snowflakes scattered across their heads, accumulated with the fallen clouds. Each one was thick with curls—some bound in braids and blue ribbons.

My gaze caught on the sapphire eyes of the head-mistress. Her stare dared to pierce through me. "There you are, lass," she greeted me with a courteous smile. Zara was settled in the light of the fireplace, dressed in a fresh satin gown. Bruises appeared on the edge of her cheekbones; a fresh scar marked her lips.

My mouth parted with the intention of speech, but not a word seemed to suffice. Delicate flames danced across my fingertips, each one with the grace of a dancer.

With a wave from the headmistress, the Highlanders cleared out of the room. A blanket of silence fell in their wake. Lachlan and Noble remained in their seats.

I walked across the floor and settled down beside the fireplace. "Where have you been?" I asked the woman in a careful tone. "What happened in the castle?"

"Power is a complicated game," Zara said. "One moment, I am the headmistress of the finest school in this realm. Soon after the persuasion of a spineless fool, I am tossed into the pit of an old dungeon."

I remained still as her gaze traveled across the room. Her shoulders slumped in a sullen manner, which indicated the depth of her broken spirit. It was difficult to place her with the confident, steadfast character of the past. I did not care to think about the manner in which she was treated. It takes a brave soul to suffer under the hands of corruption.

"I have returned with purpose," Zara raised her chin with the light of renewed hope. She addressed the entire room with that bright glint in her stare. "I've long since considered myself a mentor to each of the ladies seated beside me. I must apologize for all of the struggles that have rested upon their shoulders without proper guidance. I'm astonished by the faith and fortitude that has found a home in this place. To be sure, it stems from the resilience of these four maidens."

My sister reached out and clasped her hand around mine. Her palms were cold and covered in frost. Nevertheless, there was a trace of comfort to be found in her touch.

"We must hold on to that courage," Zara continued, "for this band of warriors will need it more than all of the sharpened arrows in the realm."

"We must discover their fatal flaw," said Ariadne. "We've all been locked in that castle for weeks. We've seen their fortress with our own eyes. There must be something to use against them."

"We already have our weapons!" Noble peered down at the book in his hands. "The High Queens of Aisling will rise against the infiltration of the Order of Birch. With your claim to power, the Gifted people are bound to see in real colors. We shall unmask the truth of my father's past, as well as the death of Sir Amulet."

"You have reading glasses?" Killian chuckled.

"Yes," Noble huffed. "And you have a tail."

"Some people will do anything for power," Zara stated, "while others consider it to be of little importance."

"Humans," said Juniper, "can be such wretched creatures. Nevertheless, we have such an extraordinary capacity for love. Perhaps that is evidence of our eternal fate."

Noble slammed his book down on the table and turned to approach me. "And I hope you have made a final decision," his words flowed in a smooth tone. "There isn't another moment to waste."

"Indeed."

"Well, then?"

"I shall accept the throne with the other girls. Our role shall be a symbolic one, as each of us serve as the face of the revolution. With her acceptance, Zara Hawthorne will act as regent to the crown. Her duties shall be transferred at the time of our eighteenth birthday. Hawthorne knows the histories of this realm far better than her students. She deserves to stand at the frontline of this battle, to finalize the decisions that will lead to the downfall of the Lennox clan. I refuse to accept the crown without her guidance."

"A wise notion," Lachlan murmured. "Although it must be considered with care."

"You trust her to make the right decisions?" Noble spoke with a hint of surprise.

"As should the entire realm," I replied. "Over the past few months, she has proven her loyalties more than once. Her intentions are driven toward the protection of the Gifted children. She seeks the light which flickers in the distance."

"I agree." Emery nodded with the other girls. "Four teenagers cannot be expected to reign alone. The guidance of the headmistress will prove beneficial. Her experience with the Order of Birch exceeds that of this entire rebellion."

"Oh, brave girls," said Zara. "Your trust is worth more than the finest silk. I've seen you grow in more ways than one. Blind ambition drives the foolish, while the soul directs the wise. It will be an honor to serve beside the throne, to restore this realm to a state of peace."

"So you accept the role of regent?" Lachlan confirmed.

"Indeed," Zara spoke with a smile. "Although I believe it will be wise to keep this matter under wraps for the time. We cannot force the formation of monarchs. Do not proclaim their position; allow it to form with their actions. A land of freedom never takes well to the establishment of rulers. These maidens must be encouraged to positions of leadership, bound in the respect of the Gifted society."

"Very well," said Noble. "This band of warriors shall be directed, for the decisions of these women are bound to restore. Our lives rest in your hands. Handle each one with care."

❧❦❦❧

I stood on the edge of the stage, with eyes raised toward the ethereal moon. That wooden platform creaked beneath me, worn from ages of abandonment. A pair of flames glowed in the center of my palms. Their performance reenacted visions of midnights past.

Moonrise lifted the spirits of the warriors. High-landers never faltered from conversation, as each one

227

spoke with a tongue of wit. Their voices bellowed with enough laughter to illuminate the darkness. I listened with a smile of contentment, for there was solace to be found in the presence of kindred spirits.

Soon enough, the old theatre seemed to reawaken. Silver moonlight swept over the broken walls. One of the elders swiped golden stripes under my lashes, in symbols to mark me with the soul of a true warrior.

A steady tune arose from somewhere in the crowd. People gathered around to light the darkness, and the platform soon boasted an entire session of traditional musicians. Their stringed instruments formed a reel to soothe anxious hearts.

The crowd shouted in delight, and children dashed across the floor with ribbons brandished high. Couples danced in and out of time to the music. At that moment, a familiar face appeared before me. His freckled cheeks curved into a dimpled grin. "May I have this dance?" Ronan reached a hand out in expectation.

I stared at him for a moment before returning the gesture. With a swift twirl and stamp of our shoes, the dance was brought to life. Music echoed with pipes to match the spirit and drums to match the heart. Not a single outsider could hear our voices in such deep woodland. We did not care about the broken silence, for it was made to shatter like glass.

Amid the swirling haze of colors and pure echoes of laughter, there was a glorious thing to behold. For while the Lennox clan followed ambition, the Guardians lived with the love of those born and unborn, strange as each one was bound to become. Between a pair of divergent forests, the theatre was a home for all. Countless constellations reminded me of the souls that linger overhead, and those lives that did not pass in vain. Despite the sorrows of the past, the Gifted people were most alive in the kindred woods.

The reel ended in a sharp tone, before the pipers picked it up once more. Ronan halted in the middle of the platform. A trickle of sweat dripped over his forehead. His deep gaze focused on mine. I didn't know what to think of his expression.

"What's happened?" I asked him.

"Nothing," he replied with a shake of his head.

"What's wrong?" I persisted as the music faded into the background. "Tell me, Ronan! Or else I'll suppose my lack of grace offends you!"

Ronan looked back at me and lowered his chin. His gaze sparkled under the stars, while a bit of laughter escaped him. "I've never seen one with such radiance." His brows raised with slight amusement, though his words did not contain a trace of it.

A chord struck against my heart. Our smiles were the first notes in the music that remained. It was the calm before the storm.

CHAPTER TWENTY-EIGHT

One week passed after that night under starlight. All the while, those memories remained with me. I hummed to the rhythm of the reel; I swayed to the steps of the dance. It held me together more than once, when all seemed to shatter before my eyes.

Christmas Eve arrived with the deepest love of the season. It brought the scent of fresh biscuits and warmth of prayers with it. If children did not wander the halls, one might've forgotten such celebrations.

Messengers travelled between the woodlands, reporting back from spies scattered across the realm. The news was seldom positive, as search parties moved closer to this side of the forest, and knights raided the dormitories of the Academy for Gifted Youth. Each armored servant sought to find four girls with elemental powers.

I was a rebel on the run—an outlander, seeker of peace, and untamable child of the Gifted realm.

That afternoon was spent on horseback as a group of archers scoped out the surrounding trails and swiftest routes to the Highlands. Lachlan told me it was a matter of precaution, to make sure the Fortress was prepared for the backlash of the Order of Birch. This statement fueled tensions. It spoke to the worst fears in my mind.

I rode across the glen without much purpose, for it seemed as though all action required a period of patience. It was too dangerous to place myself on the front lines. Ariadne and Juniper trotted beside me, while my sister's horse cantered far ahead.

The High Queens of Aisling.

I looked into their eyes and saw nothing more than girls born into a wonderous tale. Each one was a creation of the greatest love ever known. In that sense, we were no different than those from New England and the lands beyond.

"Can you believe it has been over one year since the Hanley sisters came to Aisling?" Ariadne spoke with her gaze focused on the horizon. A thin trail of smoke climbed from the chimneys of the nearest village. "It seems like a lifetime has passed since that introduction in Lancaster Hall."

"Ah, yes!" I responded with a slight chuckle. "And I remember it well enough."

"Is that so?"

231

"As I recall, the first impression gave no hint of your true character," I said. "That trunk of novels and lack of words painted the portrait of diffidence, indeed. Far too little did we know of your sharp tongue and wealth of wit."

Ariadne tossed her head back in laughter. "Things were different back then." She sighed. "Childhood was a simple time, and I am afraid these past months have pushed me away from it."

"Childhood does not last forever," said Juniper. "Although I believe the childish soul can endure for an eternity."

"Last summer brought the end of that time," I spoke in a thoughtful tone. "When I stepped into Macnas Manor, something moved within my spirit. I cannot explain it... but I suppose my powers shifted into place."

"One never feels right until their feet are planted in the soil of their rightful home," Juniper murmured.

"It was once a difficult task, to find control over the fire in my soul," I reminisced. "At times, these flames felt like a hopeless curse. I envied the control my sister possessed. The elements of water and ice seemed like such wonders in her hands. It was so difficult to master those flames, until the scope of imagination shifted. I found a renewed perspective."

"One mortal does not have the power to control nature," said Juniper, allowing her emerald eyes to reveal the glimmer of a thousand forests. "We have the power to speak with nature... and it listens to our words."

CHAPTER TWENTY-NINE

fternoon soon transformed into evening, when skies winked toward the man on the moon. A valley of starlight appeared like silver freckles across the horizon. I wandered around the dusted corridors, in search of lost thoughts. My lantern led me back to the makeshift bedchambers, where the other girls conversed beside candlelight. Their words revealed fears and dreams of the future, of the fate that continued to unfold with stories intertwined.

I crawled under their castle of laughter and blankets. It reminded me so much of the previous summer, when our friendship became more like a sisterhood. I recalled slumber parties and light-hearted ventures through the forests. Those days were simple, enough for me. I longed to go back in time, even for a single moment.

We stayed up for hours, until our eyelids refused to stay open. Unlike most nights, sleep greeted me with ease. Consciousness faded into visions of the most peculiar sort—a dark cloud of smoke, haze of orange flames, and phoenix born from the ashes.

"Have courage, dear one." A resolute voice sounded through the fire.

All at once, the world snapped back into place. A scream sounded in the distance. I opened my eyes against the heat of restless flames.

Emery stood beside the door, where a puddle of frozen water covered the ground. "Alice!" she shouted across the burning room. "Oh, please! Someone has set the Fortress ablaze. We must get out of here at once!"

I glanced around with sudden realization. Flames climbed the walls around me, each one burning over the peeled wallpaper. I slipped out of bed and looked around at the destruction. Clouds of black smoke covered the broken rooftop, while flames devoured the hardwood floors.

A figure appeared under the dark haze. An ash-covered face of freckles revealed his name to me. He grabbed my arm and pulled me down with force.

"Ronan?" I whispered.

"Come now, Alice!" The lad coughed. "Or the future of this entire realm shall perish with us."

He led me into the corridors, where smoke climbed out the open windows, which fed the flames with the breath of nature. I focused with the hope of reaching out to the fire. It was far too distracted to listen to me.

"Close the windows!" I shouted

"Are you mad?"

"Do as I tell you! Otherwise, the entire forest shall burn to the ground," I replied. "Oxygen fuels the flames."

"Right!" Emery nodded before following orders. Her arms trembled against the heat, while her fingers covered in soot and ashes. Her frantic voice did not dare to ask more.

"Where are the others?" I demanded.

"Most have escaped," Ronan assured me. "Your parents are with the Guardians; Fionn brought the other girls into the forest on horseback. Although I haven't been able to find the headmistress."

"We can't leave her!" I pulled against his grip. "She could be trapped."

"No, Alice!" said Ronan. "No one else could've made it. The rest of the Fortress has burned to the ground, and armed knights surround each side. We'll be fortunate to escape with our lives."

His words pricked my heart with guilt, which settled with terror in the pit of my stomach. A sudden wave traveled over me. It spiked the hairs across my forearms. It was a familiar sensation that sparked a series of memories.

"She's here."

"Who's here?" Ronan groaned, leading me toward a faint light in the distance.

Emery hurried before us. Her nightgown was soaked to the core. She glanced back every moment or so, as though she feared the loss of the imperishable. I caught sight of the frozen footprints in her wake.

A sudden flash illuminated the skies overhead, where a dark-haired huntress looked down upon the target. Cleona stood with a sharp expression as a storm gathered in the palm of her hands. Electric sparks danced between her fingers. A wicked grin of satisfaction split across her face.

At that moment, it dawned upon me.

"Emery, *move!*"

I leaped forward in time to pull her back as the roof collapsed. Soot and flames crashed down over our heads. Emery wrapped her arms around me. Moonlight vanished behind the smoke and debris. I closed my eyes with a painful sense of loss.

All at once, the chaos paused. A sudden weight pushed us to the ground. The moment seemed to stretch out in an unnatural manner. Memories of that previous dream entered my mind. "Have courage, dear one," the voice once told me. Perhaps it was time to heed such advice.

I glanced up at a most unusual sight. Ronan kneeled beside us with his hands raised toward the open skies. His face was scrunched in concentration. A heavy weight of wood and shattered marble hovered over our heads. The lad did not flinch as more crumbled against him. With a wave of his arms, the debris hurled against the opposite wall.

"Take my hand!" Ronan said.

I did not hesitate to follow his request. Emery held tight to my other arm. My heart was sure to be heard, as it continued to pound with the rhythm of a drum. Ronan pulled us off the ground and created a path through the smoke. Within moments, we rushed through the doors of the old theatre, into the fresh air of the woods.

Smoke faded to reveal a group of mounted knights. Each one brandished a lethal sword, prepared to follow the orders of another. Their weapons gleamed with power, akin to that of the flames. I searched for the man's face in the crowd—dark beard and ruthless gaze. A thin stream of tears escaped me. Behind those helmets of steel, each person was unrecognizable.

"Are you searching for him?"

Cleo appeared in the midst of the riders. Her gaze locked against mine. She was clothed in a scarlet cloak, hooded with the pelt of an unfortunate creature. Her black hair flowed against the wind that fed the blaze.

"What have you done?" I spoke without a trace of forgiveness.

"All that needed to be done," Cleo replied. "Your revolution is bound to perish with this forgotten place! All efforts shall be in vain."

"You are a fool without conscience," I said. "Your brother was wise to leave that old manor."

"Noble betrayed the Lennox clan," Cleo retorted. "He does not deserve to bear the name. Our mother's death set him on the edge of madness."

"You're wrong, Cleona," a voice spoke from behind me. Noble stood on the edge of the tree line. A bow and arrow was drawn between his arms. "Our mother's death set our father on the edge of madness. You were nothing more than an infant at the time, unable to remember the depression that entered his heart. He locked himself into his studies, where he discovered both the truth and lies of our linage. Something clicked in his mind, and our realities transformed into a corner of hell."

"What do you know?" Cleo shouted. "You left before he had the chance to continue the honorable work of our ancestors."

"*Honorable*?" Noble spat the word out. "The genocide of hundreds is far from an honorable endeavor. That terrible man seeks power, to gain control over his life and all that he lost in the past."

"And what does she seek?" Cleo pointed at me. "The Elementals do not deserve the role of rulers, let alone the power that comes with it."

"How does she know about that?" I murmured.

"The Guardians are not as clever as one might believe," Cleo sneered. "Not one noticed the foe that walked amongst them."

"What are you talking about?" Noble snapped.

At that moment, a figure moved near the edge of the woods. With sapphire eyes, the headmistress looked onward.

"Zara," Her name fell from my lips with hesitation. "What are you doing here? It's far too dangerous."

"Indeed," she spoke in a deep tone. Her gaze held a hint of amusement, which twisted into an unnatural grin. Her familiar features warped in a matter of seconds. I stared at the man who stood in her place. A terrible sense of defeat possessed me. It pricked like the thorns of a rosebush, like the poison of a witch.

Sir Lennox.

His smile was there the whole time. It hid behind her trustworthy countenance, and I never noticed the difference. It was a masquerade—a ruthless game.

"Hello, dear children," Lennox greeted us. He stroked a hand over his beard and approached with slight aversion. "Surprised, are we?"

"Where is the headmistress?" I demanded, unleashing the flames that burned under the surface. Each one leaped across my hands in rage. "What have you done?"

"Oh, let's see," Lennox replied. "Contrary to rumors, she was not placed in the dungeons. Hawthorne was kept in the opposite side of the castle, where the maids served her wine from a poisoned bottle. She left this realm in the same manner as her lost lover. She was nothing more than a threat to the fate of the Gifted society."

Anguish overwhelmed me. All at once, the earth seemed to spin with confusion. I gasped for the breath that refused to return. It was a lie. She couldn't be dead—not now, at the time when I needed her most.

"I've seen demons of the darkest sort," I confronted the man in a clear tone. "And not one has compared to the monster that dwells within you."

"Come now, Alice," Lennox replied with a chuckle. "Sensibility is not a crime."

"Have you gone mad?" Emery cried. "Hundreds of innocents have perished at your hands! Those Gifted children are no less valuable than anyone in this realm or beyond."

"With that I must disagree," Lennox responded. "Their rare abilities are much too dangerous and unpredictable.

Take yourselves as examples. Without real knowledge, there is no control; without reform, this realm is bound to fall into ruin. Classification of the Gifted was formed for the purpose of hierarchies. We are the rightful rulers of this land, according to the original decree of the High Kings of Aisling."

"No, Father, you're wrong!" said Noble. "And Cleona is no better than the lot of you! She wants nothing more than your worthless acceptance, and she will do anything to gain it."

"Noble," said Cleo. "You are making a terrible mistake."

"Look in the mirror, sister!" Noble replied. His fingers tightened around the string of his bow. "This realm is built with individuals. Not one is born with the same features and powers. Each one is a soul. Wolfgang Gregory developed his teachings out of hunger for power over his enemies. Our father continues to pursue the same nonsense! It has torn our clan apart, and it will do the same with the Order of Birch."

Noble did not release his arrow or lower his bow to the ground. He kept his eyes focused on his father. Anger burned across his face. It was not difficult to notice the adrenaline that rushed through him.

Sir Lennox wavered on the edge of confrontation, though the knights focused on his protection. When it came down to it, the coward was bound to use his daughter as a shield.

"I implore you to think with reason," Noble spoke to his sister once again. "You know the truth—how that man promised to hand his infant over to a wretched witch. That poor child was you, the final memory of his beloved wife."

"*Shut up!*"

A flash of movement caught my attention. It came from the forest, where a dark horse waited behind the trees. *Niamh.* She tossed her head once more to beckon me. Her hooves pawed at the ground with impatience.

While the others spoke in cold tones, an ember floated between us. Emery turned to look at me with a ghostly expression. I nodded toward the mare and stepped back with caution.

At once, the Lennox girl snapped her head in our direction. Her hand tossed out a surge of electric sparks, which did not reach far enough to harm her enemies. Our hairs stood rigid against her powers.

A bit of laughter escaped me.

Cleona recoiled, bowing her head with strength never seen before. A faint light seemed to disappear from her countenance. Electric storms formed between her clenched hands. A terrible realization dawned upon me.

That old voice returned to mind with one commandment. "Give freedom to the fire," the whisper flowed over the wind.

A flash of silver light collided with the heat of flames. All else faded out of focus, as an unbearable brilliance claimed our surroundings. The earth trembled underfoot, caught up in the battle of elements. I closed my eyes and screamed against the forces of nature.

A hand reached out to touch my arm. It was gentle and ever so familiar. It pulled back in a sudden manner as the light faded.

"Ronan!" I shrieked through the dark clouds. "Oh, please answer me!"

I fell to the ground and searched without sight. When the layers of smoke cleared, those knights were nowhere to be found. Cleona and Sir Lennox had vanished as well. Their footprints were mere ghosts in the remains of the Fortress. A large burn branded into the earth. Heaps of ash and rubble scattered across that hollow in the woodland.

I turned toward a horrific sight, and soon choked on the panic in my voice. Ronan sprawled across the snow with a distant sort of expression. Flames danced across his shoulders and over his limbs. When he came to terms, the lad looked around without much surprise. The fire did not burn through his attire; rather, it teased him like a child.

"I am covered in flames," said Ronan, "and not a single one burns."

I stared at him for a moment. His gaze was deep enough to fall into, like a rabbit hole to the land of wonders. He'd fallen long ago, and I was bound to follow him.

"Take my hand!"

Ronan did not hesitate to oblige the request. The flames vanished as he laced his fingers around mine. With a bit of strain, I lifted him from the ground. Ronan reached out and pulled me into an embrace. I watched him with care, while the slightest trace of laughter faded into sobs.

"Where have they gone?"

Ronan shrugged after a moment. "To prepare for battle, one might suppose."

We stood for a moment against the silence. Winter's snow fell over blackened soot and ashes. Each flake promised to cover the pain of treason. The mere sight pricked my spirit with a sense of loss. Days ago, the old theatre brimmed with ballads of the finest sort. Love and laughter filled those halls, to remind us that freedom was worth the risk. Those moments faded into memories that might've been mistaken for a dream.

Noble hoisted my sister onto the back of the dappled mare, and I followed without his assistance.

"Very well then," I spoke in soft tones. "Prepare to meet them on the battlefield, with swords and arrows drawn."

CHAPTER THIRTY

We rode through the woodlands, until the pathless soil lifted toward the hillside, and the forest fell far behind. A castle rose in the distance, crowned in banners of blue-and-white. There was a trace of hope there, behind the walls of stained glass and cobblestone. A chorus of ravens called out over the moorland.

We reached the towering entrance in time. A heavy silence covered the castle in ease. I attempted to suppress the fear in my heart, for there was no telling if the knights had returned to the school.

Noble reached out to knock on the wood, and the doors opened before he had the chance. An old friend peeked out from a crack between the doors. Her iridescent gaze crinkled around the edges, with a smile that warmed our frozen cheeks. It flashed with the colors of the rising sun—the light of a new dawn.

"Violet Holloway," I greeted the lass.

"At your service," she replied before throwing open the doors. "Step forward at once, Majesties! This winter is far too cold for my liking."

The Academy for Gifted Youth greeted me with the warmth of a hearth. Not long ago, I stood in the entrance hall for the first time. It became a sort of safe haven, a shelter in times of crisis. Reflections of chandeliers glimmered across the marble floors—bright opals and rough ambers. Each source of light held an unbroken promise.

"Alice, Emery!" startled voices sounded around the nearest corner. Ariadne and Juniper rushed into the hall. Their bare feet tapped across the dusted floors. A sharp breath escaped both of them at the sight of us—two girls with wild hair and fearless hearts.

"Oh, my stars!" Juniper exclaimed. "You've survived."

More footsteps followed after them, until the entrance hall brimmed with Gifted students and professors. Several Highlanders and Guardians walked amongst them. The scars of battle covered their bodies. Droplet faeries tended to the wounded, with baskets of fresh herbs and cloth.

My parents pushed their way to the front of the crowd, in order to have a better look at us. The pair rushed forward and gathered their daughters in an eternal embrace. A huddle of fair skin and tears—the Hanley clan was home at last.

"Oh, my dear girls," Mother spoke as tears streamed down her face. She kissed our foreheads with impatience. "You are *safe*!"

"We've been so worried," said Father. "Lachlan rescued us from the Fortress, moments before the northern side collapsed. There was no time to turn back and search, for the rest of the structure was prepared to fall with it. He promised... he promised you were safe from harm."

"I'll never be safe from harm," I whispered. "Some things aren't meant to be."

"You're safe in this castle." Killian appeared in the midst of the crowd. "The Academy for Gifted Youth stands as a renewed fortress. Sir Lennox would not dare to wage war on children of the most influential clans, no matter their position of classification."

"After all his crimes," said Emery, "I can never be sure."

"She's gone," I whispered. "Hawthorne has been poisoned, and this entire revolution shall fall without her guidance."

"Do not underestimate your strength," said Killian. "And never underestimate that of the headmistress."

"You suppose she survives?" Ariadne huffed.

"I believe in her word more than that of the Lennox clan," the fox responded.

"Rest here, for now," Fionn spoke as he stepped forward with the others. "A great battle looms on the horizon."

"In time, it shall meet us," Noble murmured. "And our swords will raise toward the skies."

At that moment, the castle hall illuminated with the shades of sunrise. I turned toward the open doors and looked out over the fields that rolled onward. Thin shadows danced under the clouds, which made way for the radiance of dawn.

As I looked out over that vast horizon, a wondrous thought came to mind. It promised to lead me into the future. For light will always penetrate darkness.

ABOUT THE AUTHOR

Erin Forbes discovered her passion for literature at a very early age. Since the date of her first publication, her work has spread to readers across the globe, and her books have developed an international fanbase. She is known for her vivid descriptions and fantastical fiction.

When she is not reading and writing, Erin enjoys art, nature, music, dance, and riding her horse. She lives on a small farm in the Hudson Valley of New York.

Follow her on social media!
@erinforbesauthor and @fireandicebookseries

ACKNOWLEDGEMENTS

This novel is a wild creature, a beast that once escaped the bounds of imagination. Each word is rooted in the heritage, culture, and essence of this life. Each character reflects one of this world. This book contains the raw emotions of a nineteen-year-old woman. It was an adventure to write, complete with laughter, tears, and unfiltered smiles. Handle it with care.

A list of individuals must be acknowledged in regard to the success of this work. A large bundle of appreciation goes to my parents. Without their unwavering support, this series would not exist. Thanks to my siblings—Kaitlin, Siobhan, and John Patrick. Thanks to the team of editors who shine each sentence to perfection. Thanks to Jenny, the graphic designer who brought this realm to life in the form of a map. Thanks to the founding members of the original teen author squad—Brittney Kristina, Millie Florence, Kalan Olivia, and several others.

Thanks to those friends that pulled me through the first semester of college. Without their support and distractions, this novel might not exist. Oona, Kiernan, Róisín, and Beca—I'm talking to you!

The final thanks goes to all of my readers. With your endless support and enthusiasm, this fictional world has become so real.

Go raibh míle maith agaibh, mo chairde!

May you always find a home in Aisling.

CPSIA information can be obtained
at www.ICGtesting.com
Printed in the USA
FFHW022032220419
51914914-57341FF

9 780999 771938